The Wanderer's Havamal

The Wanderer's Havamal

Translated and Edited, with Old Norse
Text and Related Texts, by

JACKSON CRAWFORD

Hackett Publishing Company, Inc.
Indianapolis/Cambridge

24 23 22 21   4 5 6 7

The fourth printing introduces to the glossary Old Norse spellings, in parentheses, of anglicized names used in this translation.

For further information, please address
   Hackett Publishing Company, Inc.
   P.O. Box 44937
   Indianapolis, Indiana 46244-0937

   www.hackettpublishing.com

Cover design by E. L. Wilson and Brian Rak
Interior design by E. L. Wilson
Composition by Aptara, Inc.

Library of Congress Cataloging-in-Publication Data
Names: Crawford, Jackson, translator.
Title: The wanderer's Hávámal / translated, with Old Norse text and related texts,
   by Jackson Crawford.
Other titles: Hávámal. English | Hávámál.
Description: Indianapolis : Hackett Publishing Company, Inc. 2019. | Includes
   bibliographical references. | Text in English and Old Norse on facing page. | Summary:
   "The Havamal is an Old Norse poem attributed to the god Odin. Theory suggests that
   it was composed orally likely in the 900s AD in Norway. This translation by eminent
   scholar Jackson Crawford has the English translation in verse on facing pages with the
   Old Norse. Included also are commentary on the translational choices, related texts, and
   a glossary of names"—Provided by publisher.
Identifiers: LCCN 2019020338 | ISBN 9781624668357 (paperback)
   ISBN 9781624668425 (hardback)
Subjects: LCSH: Hávámál.
Classification: LCC PT7236.A31 2019 | DDC 839/.61—dc23
LC record available at https://lccn.loc.gov/2019020338

Hardback Library of Congress Control Number: 2019909190

The paper used in this publication meets the minimum requirements of American National
Standard for Information Sciences—Permanence of Paper for Printed Library Materials,
ANSI Z39.48–1984.

To Travis,

     in all your wanderings west

Contents

Foreword and Acknowledgments

Both of my translations of *Hávamál*, the "regular" translation in the style of my other Eddic translations, and the *Cowboy Hávamál*, have appeared earlier in *The Poetic Edda: Stories of the Norse Gods and Heroes* (Hackett, 2015). For several years since the publication of that book, readers have requested a standalone edition of *Hávamál*, ideally with the Old Norse text included. This volume aims to satisfy that demand, with the addition of light explanatory commentary on the Old Norse text, and a few other translations of Old Norse works that are not in the *Poetic Edda* but that shed important light on Óðin and his Valkyries.

Additionally, since completing the original version of my *Hávamál* translation in 2010, I have benefitted from another nine years of reading, researching, and teaching *Hávamál*, and I am happy to have an opportunity to refine my translation where new facts have come to my attention or new observations have struck me. Overall, more such refinements have seemed necessary in my translations of the mysteriously worded stanzas in the latter half of the poem than in my translations of the proverbs in the first half. Where such refinements have been made, often they have reflected an attempt to let the English translation match more exactly with the wording of the original, leaving more of my own interpretation to the Commentary.

The text of *Hávamál* is more complicated than it might appear at first glance, and so the chance to present the Old Norse text and a commentary on it, for those who want to understand what choices I have made in the translation, is a welcome supplement. I also particularly hope that the Old Norse text and the commentary on it prove useful to readers who aspire to read *Hávamál* in Old Norse.

I am grateful to Brian Rak and Liz Wilson at Hackett for their help at every stage of this work. During the completion of this project, I have also been happy to enjoy the kindness and encouragement of many friends, particularly De Lane Bredvik and Gordon and Dian Bredvik; Taylor Flint Budde; Carl Day, Jenn Green, and Skylar Day; Merlin and Barb Heinze; Faith Ingwersen; Peter and Marilyn Llewellyn; and Matthew T. Mossbrucker. The title of this work was the fitting suggestion of Stella Bostwick, whose assistance this year has helped save hours of my time for this and other projects. At the proofs stage, the invaluable counsel of Luke Annear, Luke Gorton, Vicki Grove, Bri Panasenco, Autumn Torres, and Reggie Young aided me. And if *Hávamál* reminds us to be friends to those who are friends to us, I have centuries left to repay Joe and Candy Turner.

My thanks to Claire, Grandma, Kerri, Dad, and Mom for good will, and to Katherine, for helping me write some of the finest pages in my life's chapters. And of course, it was Papa, June Crawford, whose wisdom and example still help me find the trail. I carry the fire as best I can, having seen him carry it high to the summit.

The mistakes and infelicities in this book are, of course, attributable to me alone.

Jackson Crawford
Sheridan, Wyoming
July 24, 2019

Stanzas 31–50 of *Hávamál* from Page 04r of the *Codex Regius*. Image courtesy of the Stofnun Árna Magnússonar í íslenskum fræðum.

Introduction

In a Nutshell

Hávamál is an Old Norse poem attributed to the god Óðin himself, and preserved together with other poems about the Norse gods and heroes in a collection called the *Poetic Edda*, written down in Iceland in ca. AD 1270. Linguistic evidence, as well as the pagan contents of the poem, suggests that it was composed orally at a much earlier time, probably in the 900s AD in Norway. The title *Hávamál* may be translated "Words of the High One," or potentially "Words of the One-Eyed," either one a reference to its authorship by Óðin. *Hávamál* is largely made up of stanzas that use pithy, concrete language to encourage wise and practical living, but also contains the only extant account of Óðin's mysterious sacrifice of himself to himself, as well as an account of his magical capabilities.

The Origins and Structure of Hávamál

Hávamál is attested in only one manuscript that has survived from the Old Norse period, the *Codex Regius* of the *Poetic Edda*, written down ca. AD 1270 in Iceland. For a work that nearly did not reach the modern age, it has achieved a certain fame in the early twenty-first century, often billed as a "Viking code of ethics," though that way of looking at it does little justice to the complex contents of this poem or to the universal character of its advice. More than a simple list of commandments, *Hávamál* uses clever imagery and succinct metaphors to encourage a patient, practical, and cynical frame of mind that was probably no more ordinary in the Viking Age than it is today. Foremost among the poem's values is its emphatic call for moderation—in drink, food, love, wisdom, and talk, among other pleasures—but never for abstinence from them. *Hávamál* is resolutely a poem of this world, of enduring its hardships rather than of withdrawing from them.

Three-quarters of the poem's stanzas are taken up with this kind of general advice, but the poem also covers some events in Óðin's life, as well as his skills with magic and the runes. Because the poem dramatically changes subject, style, and poetic meter several times, and because even linguistic evidence suggests that at least some stanzas were composed much earlier than others,[1] there are few modern scholars who accept the notion that *Hávamál* was originally composed as one continuous text (unlike most of the other poems in the *Poetic Edda*, which tend to be internally consistent in style and narrative). While the specific dividing lines between its constituent parts are debated, there is broad consensus that the poem can be broken into five or six portions that probably each have a separate origin in the oral literature of the Viking Age or the centuries immediately following.

The first part, traditionally called *Gestaþáttr*, "Guests' Portion," comprises roughly stanzas 1–81 (though st. 73, 80, and 81 are not in the same *ljóðaháttr* meter as the others, which argues that they might be later insertions by the compiler of *Hávamál*). These stanzas comprise the "classic" *Hávamál* most readers will remember, concerned

---

1. See, for example, in the Commentary under the notes on st. 32 and 106.

with advice of a worldly, often world-weary nature, delivered with a wry sense of humor and a talent for skillful and sometimes belittling metaphor. The social world of these stanzas is faithless, violent, and surprisingly secular—death is the end, we read in different words again and again, and the dead are of no use to anyone; a dead man is lucky to have a son to raise a stone in his memory, or to leave a good reputation, but the afterlife is mentioned nowhere. In fact, there is little of a supernatural or even magical nature in these stanzas, and the only solid hint that the author is Óðin is a reference to drinking with Gunnloð (a tale told in slightly more detail in the next section, *Dǿmi Óðins*). Intriguingly, the description of a forested physical world, the aristocratic titles that are used, and a few words and phrases that survive in Norwegian dialects but not in Modern Icelandic, together suggest that *Gestapáttr* originated in Viking-Age Norway, not in the nearly treeless, proto-republican world of early medieval Iceland where it would later be written down.

The second portion is sometimes called *Dǿmi Óðins*, literally "Óðin's Examples" but often called "Óðin's Love Adventures" in English. These stanzas, roughly 82–110, offer reflections on the mutual betrayals of the sexes in love affairs, with the love of the unfaithful compared in a long list to other things that cannot be trusted. But some of these stanzas also reveal a tolerant attitude toward the foolishness that love can inspire, and even the most cynical stanzas do not go so far as to promote celibacy. Like in *Gestapáttr*, the counsel that we must distrust others never becomes an admonition that we must disengage from others. Also like *Gestapáttr*, the physical world described is more Norwegian than Icelandic, and some key vocabulary items (e.g., *páfjall* "mountain in thaw" in st. 90) have cognates in Norwegian dialects but not in Icelandic. After delivering his advice on love, Óđin goes on to tell of two occasions on which he courted women, once failing (with "Billing's daughter," whoever she and Billing are), and once succeeding (with Gunnlod, the guardian of the mead Óđrerir that makes its drinker into a poet).

This is the most fragmented portion of the text; beyond the two stories about Óđin's encounters with women (st. 95–102 and 104–10) and the long list of things not to trust (st. 85–87 and 89), there is little beyond a vague focus on love and distrust that unifies the other stanzas, which are in various different meters and probably come from different poems. Scholars are also divided about whether the two love adventures were two originally separate poems about Óđin's love life, or whether they form a unified composition.

After these adventures, the third part of *Hávamál*, labeled *Loddfáfnismál* ("Words of/for Loddfáfnir") already in early-modern paper manuscripts, returns once again to wide-ranging advice, sharing wisdom on subjects as disparate as relieving oneself and protection from witches. Almost every stanza in this section, ranging from 111 to 137, opens with the same repeated four lines, beginning *Ráðum'k þér, Loddfáfnir* . . . "I counsel you, Loddfáfnir . . ." Any clues about who this Loddfáfnir might be are completely lost, and his name's apparent meaning (perhaps "young embracer") offers no help in establishing who or what he might have been. As the first stanza of this section, stanza 111, is marked out like the beginning of a new poem with a large initial capital in the *Codex Regius* manuscript, it is printed the same way in this volume.

Rúnatal "Count/Account of Runes" comprises stanzas 138–45, opening with two stanzas that enigmatically describe Óđin's sacrifice of himself to himself on a tree that is usually interpreted as Yggdrasil, the great ash tree whose roots reach into the major realms of the Norse mythic cosmos. The following stanzas are even more obscure, relating Óðin's learning of spells and some assorted lore about the runes.

The runes are letters in one of several related alphabets that were used to write early Germanic languages, including Old Norse. The particular runic alphabet used in writing Old Norse was the Younger Futhark. The Younger Futhark was an alphabet of sixteen letters that had developed in Scandinavia by ca. AD 700 from the twenty-four-letter Elder Futhark (in other countries where runes were used, such as England, the runes increased rather than decreased in number). While the runes and the ability to write them were clearly held in reverence in the Old Norse period (see, for example, st. 80), we have no specific information about how they might have been used in magic other than in writing out a spell (as alluded to, for example, in st. 151); modern books about rune magic are based more on their authors' speculation than explicit instructions in our surviving Old Norse sources. One popular misconception is that poems such as *Hávamál* were written in runes; in fact, all surviving works of Old Norse literature from Iceland were written in the Roman alphabet. *Rúnatal* is thus a work that speaks about runes rather than in or through them.

The final section, traditionally called *Ljóðatal* "Count/Account of Songs," concludes *Hávamál* with Óðin's account of his eighteen magic spells. Many of these correlate closely with magical actions he is said to perform elsewhere in Norse literature, such as in Snorri Sturluson's *Saga of the Ynglings (Ynglinga saga)*, where Snorri says that

"With words alone, he [Óðin] knew how to put out a fire or calm the waves, and he could turn the wind whatever direction he wanted. . . . And sometimes he woke dead men up out of the earth, or sat down under the hanged,"[2] which seems to refer to the spells in *Hávamál* stanzas 152, 154, and 157.

In some early-modern paper manuscripts of *Hávamál* copied (directly or indirectly) from the *Codex Regius* manuscript, the *Rúnatal* and *Ljóðatal* sections are grouped together under the subheading *Rúnatalsþáttr Óðins* "Portion about Óðin's Account of Runes" or *Rúnaþáttr Óðins* "Óðin's Portion about Runes." While there is no such subheading on this or any other section in the *Codex Regius*, the *Codex Regius* does mark out the beginning of stanza 138 with a large initial capital, a situation that has been reproduced in the poem as printed in this volume.

It is not hard to see why these five or six constituent poems were brought together under one title in the manuscript, as they all concern the kind of wisdom and lore traditionally associated with the god Óðin. Partly because of this, however, dating the poem(s) is not easy; most of the individual stanzas themselves are so self-contained that they could have been passed down independently of one another. Several individual stanzas contain words or grammar that point to a fairly archaic stage of the language (such instances are often pointed out in the Commentary in this volume), and the famous first two lines shared by stanza 76 and stanza 77 (*Deyr fé, / deyja frændr . . .* "Cows die, / family die . . .") show up also in the poem *Hákonarmál*,

---

2. The translation quoted is from my upcoming translation of Snorri Sturluson's *Prose Edda*; that volume will also include *Ynglinga saga*.

which can be confidently dated to AD 961. References to cremation (for example, in st. 81) imply an origin in the 900s or earlier, as only burial was practiced in early Christian Norway and Iceland. On the other hand, the distrustful attitude toward sex in *Dǿmi Óðins* has been taken by some to show Christian influence, though this argument seems unpersuasive in light of the fact that sex is not necessarily *discouraged* if the potential dangers of sexual relations are acknowledged, any more than walking in the woods is discouraged by acknowledging the dangers of wild animals.

As to the compiling of these poems into one poem called *Hávamál*, the best that can be said is that this probably occurred before about AD 1200, as the only manuscript in which *Hávamál* is preserved, the *Codex Regius* (GKS 2365 4to) of the Poetic Edda, was copied around AD 1270 from an exemplar written between around AD 1200 and 1240 (the dating of the exemplar is based on the more archaic spellings that show up haphazardly in the *Codex Regius* text, suggesting a copyist working from an older manuscript whose spelling he is trying to update while periodically "nodding off" in the process). Given the vast amount of material involved, and the favor that compilations of wisdom and lore had among medieval literati, most likely this compiling was done by an editor working in ink rather than at any point in the oral transmission of these stanzas. However, as demonstrated by Gustaf Lindblad, the spelling and even grammar of *Hávamál* is different in consistent ways from that of the other poems in the *Codex Regius* manuscript, which indicates that it was copied from a different written exemplar than any of the other poems in that manuscript were. At one time, then, *Hávamál* stood alone, and it was the editor of the *Codex*

Regius who chose to present it alongside other poems of the Norse gods.

The Word Hávamál

Although *Hávamál* was probably not composed as one work, the title is at least as old as the *Codex Regius*, as it occurs in red letters at the start of this poem on p. 3r of that manuscript.[3] *Mál* "words" is common in the titles of Old Norse poems, shared by other poems in the *Poetic Edda* such as *Grímnismál* or *Alvíssmál*. The most straightforward interpretation of the title *Hávamál* takes *háva* as the weak masculine genitive singular form of the adjective *hár* "high," thus "of the high one," an allusion to Óðin, who claims *Hár* "high one" as one of his names in the poem *Grímnismál*, stanza 46. In the poem *Hávamál* itself, the form *Háva* "of the high one" occurs in stanzas 109, 111, and 164, meaning "Óðin's."

However, in the closely related language Gothic, an adjective *haihs* meaning "one-eyed" is attested, and if it were preserved in Old Norse we would expect this adjective to have the form **hár* as well (for the change of **aih > á* in Old Norse, compare Gothic *aih* "I own" to Old Norse *á*, both from Proto-Germanic **aih*). This adjective is not otherwise attested in Old Norse, but if these two adjectives became confused because of their homophony in the Old

---

3. *Hávamál* appears on pages 3r–7v of the *Codex Regius*. Modern scholars number each leaf (the physical page) of a medieval manuscript, and call the front page of the leaf *recto* (abbreviated *r*) and the back page of the leaf *verso* (abbreviated *v*). Thus, page 3r of a medieval manuscript is equivalent to what we could call page 5 of a modern book (as it follows pages 1r, 1v, 2r, and 2v).

Norse period, it is possible that *Hár* as Óðin's name suggested at one time either "the high one" or "the one-eyed," or, in his characteristic ambiguity, both. An Old Norse cognate of Gothic *haihs* would not be expected to have a weak masculine genitive singular *háva* but rather **há(a)*, though the identical shape of other forms of the "high" adjective could result in the two adjectives absorbing inflectional forms from one another by analogy.[4] So, though the plain reading is "Words of the High One," there is a possibility that "Words of the One-Eyed" was a potential meaning of the title for its original Old Norse audience as well.

Translating the Poetry of Hávamál

Below I review the chief characteristics of the meters used in *Hávamál*, in order that the reader can identify and scan them in the original. Note that the meters of Eddic poetry in Old Norse rarely require a fixed number of syllables or a fixed rhythmic pattern (in contrast with well-known meters in traditional English poetry such as iambic pentameter or tetrameter). Instead, each line will have a certain number of stressed syllables that are counted as "lifts," with the number determined by the specific meter, and a certain pattern of alliteration among the lifts.

---

4. Old Norse and Gothic do not always agree as to what stem-class each adjective falls into. Old Norse *hár* "high" is a *wa*-stem, hence the -*v*- that appears in cases where the inflectional ending begins with a vowel (e.g., *háva*, "of the high one") but the cognate in Gothic, *hauhs* "high," is not a *wa*-stem. It also does not appear that Gothic *haihs* "one-eyed" was a *wa*-stem, based on masculine dative singular *haihamma* "(for a) one-eyed (man)," which appears in the Gothic Bible in Mark 9:47.

A lift must be a syllable with primary or secondary stress. Unlike the less predictable situation in English, all words in Old Norse have their primary stress on the first syllable, and only the first syllable of a word may take part in alliteration.[5] While they may not alliterate, other nonfinal syllables may have secondary stress and thus count as an additional lift, especially in the longer third and sixth lines of a *ljóðaháttr* stanza.[6] Consider English compound words such as *park ranger, elk hunter,* or *bird watcher,* where the first syllable (*park, elk, bird*) has the primary stress but the second syllable (*range, hunt, watch*) has secondary stress. In a similar way, in Old Norse compound words such as *langvinir,* "long-friends," *bóglimir* "bow-limbs, arms," and *orrusta* "battle," the first syllable (*lang, bóg, orr*) has primary stress and the second has secondary stress; the first syllable serves as a lift and the second may as well. In addition to stress, one of the following criteria must be true of a syllable for it to count as a lift:

1) The syllable contains a long vowel (*nýt, nás, rót*), a diphthong (*dauf, veit, meið*), or a short vowel followed by two or more consonants (*hross, holt, hjǫrð, niðr*[7]). Naturally low-stress words, especially prepositions (*undir* "under," *á* "on") and determiners or pronouns

---

5. The only exception, in which the non-initial (second) syllable of a word can take part in alliteration, is if the first syllable is the prefix *ó-* "un-," for example in *Hávamál,* st. 29, line 6: *opt sér ógott um gelr,* where *gelr* alliterates with *gott.* More often it is the prefix *ó-* itself that is the alliterating syllable, as in st. 103, line 9: *þat er ósnotrs aðal,* where *ó-* alliterates with *aðal* (any vowel alliterates with any other vowel).

6. Keep in mind that the acute marks above vowels in Old Norse (*á, é, í,* etc.) do not indicate stress but vowel length. A syllable may have a long vowel and yet be unstressed.

7. An *-r* at the end of a word following another consonant is not counted as its own syllable in Old Norse poetry (thus *niðr, ríðr, vegr,* and *haltr* are counted as monosyllabic words).

(such as *sá* "that, that one," *hann* "he," *inn* "the," and their forms), are seldom lifts, even if they contain long vowels or diphthongs, though they can act as lifts if their context in the line allows them to be stressed for emphasis.

2) The syllable contains a short vowel, followed by an unstressed syllable. Thus, *dug* in *dugir* "avails," *vin* in *vinir* "friends," and *gef* in *gefinn* "given" can act as lifts.

3) It is a naturally stressed monosyllabic word (generally a noun, adjective, or verb, or sometimes an emphatic pronoun or adverb; rarely an emphatic preposition), especially occurring at the end of a line or as the first element of a compound. Thus, *ǫl* "ale," *gel* "(I) sing," *nam* "(I) took," *þar* "there," and *hvat* "what" can act as lifts, as can the first syllable of *mjǫtviðr* "fate-tree; Yggdrasil" or *alsnotr* "all-wise; truly wise."

Most of the stanzas of *Hávamál* are in the Old Norse meter called *ljóðaháttr* ("meter of songs").[8] A typical *ljóðaháttr* stanza consists of six lines. Lines 1, 2, 4, and 5 have two lifts (rarely one) and one to four other syllables (rarely zero or up to six). Lines 1–2 and 4–5 form couplets; at least one of the lifts in line 1 alliterates with at least one of the lifts in line 2, and lines 4 and 5 are structured as a couplet in the same way. There is no coordination between the alliteration in lines 1–2 and lines 4–5. Line 3 stands alone with two, or more often, three lifts, two of which alliterate with each other (not necessarily with a lift in any other line), and line 6 is structured in the same way. Lines 3 and 6 usually have two to six other syllables, often before or adjacent to the first lift. An example (st. 92) is printed below with a

---

8. Not every stanza of *Hávamál* can be scanned in a recognizable meter, but clear examples of *ljóðaháttr* (including the *galdralag* variant) are st. 1–72, 74–79, 84, 88, 91–124, 126–28, 130, 132–36, 138, 140, and 146–64.

slash above each lift and with the first letter of each alliterating lift underlined. Note that any vowel alliterates with any other vowel (or with a syllable beginning with *j*, or sometimes *v*).

> / /
> <u>F</u>agrt skal mæla
> / /
> ok <u>f</u>é bjóða
> / / /
> sá er vill <u>f</u>ljóðs ást <u>f</u>á.
> / /
> <u>L</u>íki <u>l</u>eyfa
> / /
> ins <u>l</u>jósa mans;
> / /
> sá <u>f</u>ær er <u>f</u>rjár.

In a nine-line *ljóðaháttr* stanza such as the famous stanza 138, lines 7–8 are structured as a couplet in the same way as lines 1–2, and line 9 alliterates with itself in the same way as line 3:

> / /
> <u>V</u>eit ek at ek hekk
> / /
> <u>v</u>indga meiði á
> / / /
> <u>n</u>ætr allar <u>n</u>íu,
> / /
> geiri undaðr
> / /
> ok <u>g</u>efinn Óðni,

/   /   /
sjálfr sjálfum mér,
   /   /
á þeim meiði
    /   /
er manngi veit
        /   /
hvar's hann af rótum renn.

Ljóðaháttr is principally used for dialogue and, as in so much of *Hávamál,* for proverbial sayings. The use of consecutive *ljóðaháttr* stanzas to tell a story, as in *Hávamál* stanzas 95–102 and 104–10, is relatively uncommon.

Some of the stanzas describing magical spells are in a type of *ljóðaháttr* called *galdralag* "meter of magic," as are other stanzas without immediately apparent magical content, such as stanza 105. This meter is similar to normal *ljóðaháttr,* but adds at least one extra line of the same type as line 3 or 6 (i.e., a line with two or three lifts, at least two of which in the same line alliterate with each other). The meter also favors fewer lifts, placed late in the line. An example is stanza 149, which adds one such extra line at the end:

     /
Þat kann ek it fjórða;
    /   /
ef mér fyrðar bera
/   / /
bönd at bóglimum,
   /
svá ek gel

/   /
at ek ganga má.

     /   /
Sprettr mér af fótum fjǫturr,

/   /
en af hǫndum hapt.

The narrative poems in the *Poetic Edda* are in *fornyrðislag* ("meter of ancient sayings"), in which case the stanza consists only of paired couplets (usually four, sometimes three or five) that are paired in the same way as the first two lines of a *ljóðaháttr* stanza. Stanza 139 of *Hávamál* provides the most regular of the few examples from this poem (note that this meter favors one-lift lines more than *ljóðaháttr*):

    /   /
Við hleifi mik søldu,

    /
né við hornigi.

/   /
Nýsta ek niðr,

/   /
nam ek upp rúnar—

/   /
øpandi nam—

    /
fell ek aptr þaðan.

Other stanzas use *málaháttr* "speech meter," a modified form of *fornyrðislag* consisting of sets of paired couplets, usually three or four. The technical distinctions are complex, but a *málaháttr* line typically has a more predictable syllable count than a line in the other two meters, with two lifts and three or four other syllables, for a consistent five or six syllables in total.[9] An example is stanza 144:

> /   /
> Veiztu hvé r̲ísta skal?
> /   /
> Veiztu hvé r̲áða skal?
> /   /
> Veiztu hvé f̲á skal?
> /   /
> Veiztu hvé f̲reista skal?
> /   /
> Veiztu hvé b̲iðja skal?
> /   /
> Veiztu hvé b̲lóta skal?
> /   /
> Veiztu hvé s̲enda skal?
> /   /
> Veiztu hvé s̲óa skal?

While Old Norse meters can be successfully imitated in original English compositions, Old Norse is a much more "compact" medium of expression than English overall, requiring fewer words to express the same thought, because the language uses a rich system of inflectional endings and vowel mutations to indicate the relationships of words to one another. Old Norse also has no indefinite article

---

9. Examples of *fornyrðislag* or *málaháttr,* often a mix of the two, are st. 73, 81–83, 85–87, 89–90, 139, and 144.

(English *a, an*), and the archaic language of *Hávamál* makes little use even of the definite article (English *the*), so these words require extra space in the line in English. Because I favor communicating the meaning of an Old Norse stanza over compromising its meaning to preserve its form, I have therefore made it my practice to translate Old Norse poems into rhythmic free verse in English.

In comparing the Old Norse line by line with the English translation, bear in mind that, because much of a sentence's meaning is "coded" into endings and vowel changes, word order in Old Norse poetry is so free that it is impossible to translate words in the exact same order as they appear in the Old Norse text.

For a simple example, in English the difference between "man bites dog" and "dog bites man" is indicated entirely by word order— the noun to the left of the verb, "bites," indicates the one who did the biting. But in Old Norse, it is the form of the noun that indicates if it is the subject or object of the verb—*hundr bítr mann* "dog bites man" is equivalent in meaning to *mann bítr hundr*, where the order of the words is reversed but their forms remain the same. Conversely, *hund bítr maðr* means "man bites dog" in spite of having the same words in the same order, because the forms of the nouns have changed to indicate that *maðr* "man" is the subject now and *hund* "dog" is the object (vs. object form *mann* and subject form *hundr* in the previous example sentence).

Because the words have to be rearranged in such a way that they can form a meaningful sentence in English, readers ought not to assume that, say, the first word in the first line of a stanza in Old Norse is exactly translated by the first word in the first line of the same stanza in my facing English translation. By way of example, consider how one might translate stanza 133 into Modern English while following the same word order as the original:

Opt vitu ógǫrla	Often know imperfectly
þeir er sitja inni fyrir	those who sit inside before
hvers þeir'ru kyns er koma,	of-what those-are of-type who come,
er-at ψ svá góðr	is-not man/person so good
at galli né fylgi,	that flaw not follows,
né svá illr at einugi dugi.	nor so bad that for-nothing is-good.

The result is, at best, very artificial-looking, and at worst, a puzzle of words that English grammar is almost helpless to piece together. Therefore, the beginning reader of the Old Norse text is encouraged to consider the meaning of the whole stanza together rather than attempting to translate it word-by-word, or comparing it to my own translation in a rote word-by-word (or even line-by-line) manner. Consider stanza 133 in my finished translation:

> Those inside the house
> rarely know anything
> about the stranger who knocks at their door,
> but there is no man so good
> that he has no flaw,
> nor a man so bad he's good for nothing.

Notice that the sense of the second line in Old Norse has been moved into the first line, to reflect the fact that the subject generally appears first in the sentence in English, and the verb has accordingly been moved from the first line into the second line. I have filled in the context as well, clarifying that the scene is one of hosts inside a house—"those who sit inside before (the doors)" in the Old Norse—knowing little about "those who come." In order to evoke such a scene for the English-speaking reader, I have made this unknown visitor "the stranger who knocks at their door."

In Old Norse, proverbial wisdom is often phrased in the third person and without any stated subject whatsoever, so that *um skoðask skyli* in the third line of stanza 1 might be translated (excessively literally) as simply "should look around." However, in my translations of such stanzas (e.g., st. 35, 52, or 144), I have generally inserted the universalized second-person "you," as "you" is the normal audience for advice and proverbs in contemporary English. On occasion, I have also translated stanzas or parts of stanzas that have an explicit third-person subject *maðr* "man/person" into the second person in English, when doing so seemed less stylistically awkward or repetitive than using the third person. This is especially the case with stanzas such as stanza 19 where the Old Norse text includes what are effectively imperatives in the third person in the first half, and abruptly transitions to second person in the second half. As with all my translations, I have also freely translated the conjunctions between clauses and stanzas to insure an unmonotonous rhythm and style in English.

Note on Language and Spelling

Hávamál, and the other texts translated in this volume, were composed in Old Norse, the written language of medieval Iceland and Norway. This language, sometimes called Old West Norse, is the direct ancestor of today's Icelandic, Norwegian, and Faroese languages, and is very closely related to Old East Norse, the ancestor of Danish and Swedish. Old Norse is also a "first cousin" to other old Germanic languages, such as Gothic, Old English, and Old High German, and thus distantly related (as an "aunt" or "uncle") to modern Germanic languages such as English, German, and Dutch. Old Norse was written using the Roman alphabet (the alphabet used for English and most other Western European languages today) beginning in approximately AD 1150, with the addition of some new letters for sounds that the Roman alphabet was not designed to accommodate.

No consistent standard for spelling the language was ever developed during the Old Norse period, so there is substantial variation in spelling between manuscripts and even between different lines on the same page in one manuscript. In rendering the text of *Hávamál* in Old Norse, I have followed the usual practice among editors of Old Norse texts and normalized the spelling to that of "classical" textbook Old Norse. This standard is based on the spellings in Icelandic manuscripts from the mid-1200s, i.e., a little earlier than the *Codex Regius* itself, and is a desirable model to follow in a work such as this which aims to make the Old Norse text readable for relative beginners in the language whose dictionaries and grammars will make use of this spelling standard. Note, however, that I write the I-umlauted version of the long vowel *ó* as *ǿ*, corresponding in form with the short version of the same vowel (*ø*), while English- and German-speaking editors usually render the letter *ǿ* as *œ* (a ligature of *o+e*, easily confused with the *æ* ligature from *a+e*). The *Codex Regius* manuscript also uses the rune named *maðr*, which represents the consonant [m], in many stanzas to represent the word *maðr* "man, person." In such instances I have printed the graphically identical Greek letter ψ, which thus is not to be read as a letter but as the word *maðr*. For more details about how the Old Norse text is presented, see my prefatory remarks in the Commentary.

In the English translations in this volume, I have rendered Old Norse names in a less anglicized form than in my translation of the *Poetic Edda*.[10] The names of humans and gods are written essentially as they are in standard Old Norse, with the following modifications and considerations:

1. The letter *þ* (called "thorn"), capital form *Þ*, is rendered as *th* (thus *Þórr* becomes *Thór*, and *Þjóðreyrir* becomes *Thjóðreyrir*). The letter *þ* represents the sound of *th* in English *worth* or *breath*, but the letter is frequently mistaken for *p*.

2. The letter *ð* (called "eth"), capital form *Ð*, which in origin is a rounded medieval letter *d* with a crossbar, is rendered as a straight-backed, modern *d* with a crossbar, *đ* (thus *Óđrerir*, *Óđin*, *Gunnlod*, *Midgarđ*, *Ásgarđ*). This letter represents the sound of *th* in English *worthy* or *breathe* (not *worth* or *breath*). I use the less common straight-backed version of this letter in my English translation because the rounded version is frequently mistaken for *o*.

3. The letter *ǫ* (called "o caudata") is rendered as *o* (thus *Gunnlǫð* is rendered as *Gunnlod*). In Old Norse, the letter *ǫ* represented the sound of *o* in English *or*. This vowel has become *ö* in Modern Icelandic and usually *o* in Modern Norwegian. Some editors and

---

10. In that volume, only the twenty-six letters used in English are employed, so the length of vowels is ignored, and both *þ* and *ð* are printed as *th*. Meanwhile, I rendered the Old Norse name *Óðinn* in that book as *Odin* because of its familiarity to English readers, while in this book, consistent with the anglicization used for other names, I have written *Óđin*.

translators use Modern Icelandic *ö* here, but this encourages an anachronistic pronunciation. Unfortunately there are few fonts or digital readers that successfully render *ǫ*, and the letter is easily mistaken for *q*, but the use of plain *o* to render this vowel is not unknown from Old Norse manuscripts.

4. In accordance with the usual convention of modern translators, the *-r* that ends many names in the subject (nominative) case is removed. Old Norse is a highly inflected language, and certain endings are added to the root of a word when it performs different functions—for example, *Suttungr* is the giant's name when he is the subject of a verb ("*Suttungr* hit me"), but his name is *Suttung* without the *-r* when he is the object ("I hit *Suttung*"). This grammatical ending appears as a second *-r* or *-n* on masculine names that end in *-r* (such as *Fjalarr*) or *-n* (such as *Óðinn*), and this is removed by the same convention (thus *Fjalar, Ódin* in my translation). However, the *-r* at the end of a name is left intact when it is part of the name's root and not simply a grammatical ending; the most important name of this kind is *Baldr*. By convention, the final *-r* is also left intact in names that end in *-ir*, thus *Thjódreyrir*.

I have followed the same guidelines in rendering Old Norse place-names, but I have substituted modern place-names when these are available in order to facilitate comparison with good modern maps (thus Norwegian *Agder* and *Hordaland*, rather than Old Norse *Agdir* and *Hordaland*). In dealing with some well-known names where an English rendering of the Old Norse word is already widespread and popular, I have used that instead of directly transliterating the Old Norse word according to the guidelines above: thus, I write *Valhalla* and *Valkyrie* instead of the more authentic or consistent *Valholl* and *Valkyrja*.

In the Commentary, I have generally spelled names (including the titles of Old Norse poems) according to these rules of anglicization, unless I am specifically discussing an Old Norse word or name per se, thus, in my comments on stanza 80:

> Óðin is identified in the Old Norse text of this stanza as *Fimbulþulr*. *Fimbul* means "mighty, terrible," often with a sense of the supernatural; the *fimbulvetr* is the "mighty winter" that will accompany Ragnarok, the death of the gods, and in stanza 140 Óðin declares he knows nine *fimbulljóð* "mighty songs," i.e., magical spells (but in st. 103, *fimbul-fambi* is simply "a (terrible) fool"). For remarks on the meaning of *þulr*, see my comments on stanza 111, below.

The italicized words are spelled out fully in Old Norse, because I am drawing attention to and commenting on the words themselves. Meanwhile, the names Óðin and Ragnarok are anglicized according to the rules outlined above because I am discussing Óðin as a being and Ragnarok as an event, not the Old Norse words *Óðinn* or *Ragnarǫk*.

Pronunciation

The pronunciation of Old Norse in the mid-1200s AD (roughly speaking, the time when *Hávamál* was written down) can be reconstructed with great confidence using the tools of historical linguistics, and this reconstructed medieval pronunciation is easier to learn and more historically authentic than the Modern Icelandic pronunciation favored by many today.

In reading Old Norse aloud, a few ground rules ought to be kept in mind. The accent is always on the first syllable of a word, thus

ÓÐ-re-rir, not *óð-RE-rir*, *LODD-fáf-nir*, not *lodd-FÁF-nir*, and so on. The Old Norse pronunciation of most consonants is similar enough to the Modern English pronunciation to require no comment. The most important facts to note are these:

ð (or in the translation, *đ*) is pronounced as the English *th* in *worthy* or *breathe* (not *worth* or *breath*); thus *Óðinn* is pronounced *OTHE-inn*, with a first syllable that rhymes with English *loathe* or *clothe* (not *loath* or *oath*).

f is pronounced as *v* when following a vowel; thus, the name *Loddfáfnir* is pronounced close to *LODD-fov-near*.

g is pronounced as in *go*, never with the sound of *j* as in *gin*; thus, the second syllable of *Reginn* is like that of *begin*, not like the liquor *gin*.

h can occur in the combinations *hj* (*hjálp, hjarta*), *hl* (*hlátr, hlýðir*), *hr* (*Hróptr, hrein*), and *hv* (*hvat, hverr*). *Hj* is pronounced with the *hy* sound of the *h* in English *Houston* or *hue*, and *hv* probably with the *hw* sound of older American English *wh* in *what* or *whale* (see also *j* and *v*, below). The sounds of *hl* and *hr* are, similarly, produced by pronouncing the *h* in English *he* followed by an *l* or *r* before the vowel.

j is pronounced as the English *y* in *young*, or the German *j* in *ja*; thus, *Jǫtunheimr* is pronounced *YAWT-une-hame-r*. The sequence *hj* is pronounced *hy* as the *h* in English *Houston* or *hue*.

r is a trill, as in Scottish English or Spanish. In many words, final *-r* after another consonant constitutes a separate syllable, not unlike the way that the final syllable in American English *water* or *bitter* is really only a syllabic *r* pronounced without a "true" vowel before it. However, as noted above, this final *-r* is not treated as a separate syllable in poetic scansion.

s is pronounced as in *bass*, never with the sound of *z* as in *has*; thus, *Áslaug* is pronounced *OSS-loug*, not *OZ-loug*.

þ (*th* in the translation) is pronounced as the English *th* in *worth* or *breath* (not *worthy* or *breathe*), thus *Þórr* (*Thór*) is correctly pronounced nearly as it is usually pronounced in English (his name is not pronounced like *tore* or *tour*, as it is in modern Scandinavian languages or German).

v is pronounced as the English *v* in *very*. It is likely that a *v* after another consonant was pronounced as *w* (a pattern not unknown in modern languages, for example in the pronunciation of the letter *w* in some dialects of Afrikaans), so *hvat* would begin with the *hw* sound of older American English "what," and *svá* would be pronounced roughly as *swaw*.

Vowels without the acute length mark (´) are pronounced as in Spanish, so *a* is the *o* of American English *got*, *e* is the *e* of *pet*, *i* is the *ee* of *feet*, *o* is approximately the *oa* in *boat* (pronouncing this word with an Upper Midwest accent will be nearer the actual Scandinavian pronunciation), and *u* is the *oo* of *boot*. The vowel *y* is similar to *u*, but farther forward in the mouth, like the German *ü* or the vowel in a "surfer" pronunciation of *dude* or *tune*. The letter *y* is not used as a consonant in Old Norse (see *j*, above). The vowel *æ* is pronounced as the *a* in *cash*, and the vowel *ø* has a pronunciation somewhat like the *i* in *bird* (more authentically, the German or Swedish *ö* or the Norwegian or Danish *ø*). A vowel with the acute length mark (´) is pronounced with the same sound as the equivalent unmarked vowel, but the syllable lasts a few fractions of a second longer (compare the words *hat* and *had* in English, where the vowel is longer in the second word than in the first). The exception is long *á*, which is pronounced with more rounding of the lips than the short vowel, similar to the *o* in many older American pronunciations of *on*, or to the *o* in a northern New Jersey pronunciation of *coffee*. The short version of the same "coffee" vowel is written *ǫ* in classical Old Norse.

The diphthong *au* is pronounced like the *ou* of *house*, while *ei* is the *ai* of *rain*. The diphthong *ey* is somewhat similar to the *oy* in *boy*, if pronounced with pursed lips (a more authentic parallel would be the Norwegian *øy*).

Further Reading

The following texts may benefit the student who wishes to delve deeper in the study of *Hávamál*, or Norse mythology and language more broadly.

Barnes, Michael, and Anthony Faulkes. *A New Introduction to Old Norse*. 3 vols. Viking Society for Northern Research, 2008.

> The most accessible and complete resource for learning the Old Norse language that is available at this time.

Crawford, Jackson (translator). *The Poetic Edda: Stories of the Norse Gods and Heroes*. Hackett, 2015.

> Contains my original translation of *Hávamál* into English, as well as my translations of the other poems of the *Poetic Edda*, including *Voluspá* and *Grímnismál*.

Crawford, Jackson (translator). *The Saga of the Volsungs, with The Saga of Ragnar Lothbrok*. Hackett, 2017.

> *The Saga of the Volsungs* is a major Norse saga in which Óđin plays a crucial part as instigator, advisor, tormenter, and killer.

Evans, David A. H., ed. *Hávamál*. Viking Society for Northern Research, 1986.

>An influential academic edition of the Old Norse text. Contains a wide-ranging introduction and a thorough commentary.

Gísli Sigurðsson, ed. *Eddukvæði*. 2nd Ed. Mál og menning, 2014.

>A superb edition of the Old Norse text of the Poetic Edda (in Modern Icelandic orthography). Includes a detailed commentary in Modern Icelandic.

Jesch, Judith. *Ships and Men in the Late Viking Age*. Boydell & Brewer, 2001.

>An informative study of Old Norse vocabulary in the earliest datable texts.

Jesch, Judith. *The Viking Diaspora*. Routledge, 2015.

>An unparalleled examination of society in the Viking Age.

Jónas Kristjánsson and Vésteinn Ólason, eds. *Eddukvæði I: Goðakvæði*. Hið íslenzka fornritafélag, 2014.

>Edited texts of the Poetic Edda, with thorough commentary in Modern Icelandic.

Liberman, Anatoly. *In Prayer and Laughter*. Paleograph, 2016.

>A collection of essays on Norse and Germanic mythology by one of the most influential and insightful recent scholars on the language of the Eddas.

Lindblad, Gustaf. *Studier i Codex Regius av Äldre Eddan*. Gleerup, 1954.

>The definitive study of the *Codex Regius* manuscript.

McKinnell, John. *Essays on Eddic Poetry*. University of Toronto Press, 2014.

>A wide-ranging collection; includes several influential articles on *Hávamál*.

Mitchell, Stephen. *Witchcraft and Magic in the Nordic Middle Ages*. University of Pennsylvania Press, 2013.

>An important study of the concept of magic in early medieval Scandinavia, including a review of Óðin's magical knowledge as revealed in *Hávamál* and elsewhere.

Saxo Grammaticus (author), Karsten Friis-Jensen (editor), and Peter Fisher (translator). *Gesta Danorum (The History of the Danes), Volume I*. Clarendon Press, 2015.

> A work of medieval scholarship by the Danish historian Saxo Grammaticus, who died in approximately AD 1220. Includes some myths about Óðin ("Othinus") found nowhere else.

Snorri Sturluson (author) and Anthony Faulkes (translator). *Edda*. Everyman's Library, 1995.

> A translation not of the *Poetic Edda* but the *Prose Edda*, a work by Snorri Sturluson (1179–1241), who attempted in this book to make a coherent whole out of the Norse myths current in his time. This translation is the best currently available in English.

Hávamál

1.   Gáttir allar
       áðr gangi fram,
um skoðask skyli,
um skyggnask skyli—
því at óvíst er at vita
hvar óvinir
sitja á fleti fyrir.

2.   Gefendr heilir!
Gestr er inn kominn,
hvar skal sitja sjá?
Mjǫk er bráðr,
sá er á brǫndum skal,
síns um freista frama.

3.   Elds er þǫrf,
þeim's inn er kominn,
ok á kné kalinn.
Matar ok váða
er manni þǫrf,
þeim er hefir um fjall farit.

4.   Vatns er þǫrf,
þeim er til verðar kømr,
þerru, ok þjóðlaðar,
góðs um ǿðis—
ef sér geta mætti,
orðs ok endrþǫgu.

1. At every doorway
    before you enter,
    you should look around,
    you should take a good look around—
    for you never know
    where your enemies
    might be seated within.

2. Hail to a good host!
    A guest has come inside,
    where should he sit?
    He is impatient,
    standing on the threshold,
    ready to try his luck.

3. He needs a fire,
    the one who has just come in,
    his knees are shivering.
    Food and dry clothes
    will do him well,
    after his journey over the mountains.

4. He needs water,
    the one who has just arrived,
    dry clothes, and a warm welcome
    from a friendly host—
    and if he can get it,
    a chance to listen and be listened to.

5. Vits er þǫrf
    þeim er víða ratar;
    dælt er heima hvat.
    At augabragði verðr
    sá er ekki kann
    ok með snotrum sitr.

6. At hyggjandi sinni
    skyli-t maðr hrøsinn vera,
    heldr gætinn at geði,
    þá er horskr ok þǫgull
    kømr heimisgarða til.
    Sjaldan verðr víti vǫrum,
    því at óbrigðra vin
    fær ψ aldregi
    en mannvit mikit.

7. Inn vari gestr
    er til verðar kømr,
    þunnu hljóði þegir,
    eyrum hlýðir
    en augum skoðar—
    svá nýsisk fróðra hverr fyrir.

8. Hinn er sæll
    er sér um getr
    lof ok líknstafi.
    Ódælla er við þat
    er ψ eiga skal
    annars brjóstum í.

5.   A man needs wisdom
        if he plans to wander widely;
        life is easier at home.
        He'll be laughed at
        if he sits among the wise
        and has nothing to say.

6.   A wise man
        is not showy about his wisdom;
        he guards it carefully.
        He is silent when he comes
        to a stranger's home.
        Harm seldom befalls the watchful man,
        for you can never have
        a more faithful friend
        than a good supply of wisdom.

7.   The watchful guest,
        when he arrives for a meal,
        should keep his mouth shut,
        listening with his ears
        and watching with his eyes—
        that is how the wise man finds his way.

8.   A man is happy
        if he finds praise and friendship
        within himself.
        You can never be sure
        of where you stand
        in someone else's heart.

9.   Sá er sæll
       er sjálfr um á
       lof ok vit meðan lifir.
       Því at ill ráð
       hefir ψ opt þegit
       annars brjóstum ór.

10.   Byrði betri
       berr-at ψ brautu at
       en sé mannvit mikit.
       Auði betra
       þykkir þat í ókunnum stað—
       slíkt er válaðs vera.

11.   [Byrði betri
       berr-at ψ brautu at
       en sé mannvit mikit.]
       Vegnest verra
       vegr-a hann velli at
       en sé ofdrykkja ǫls.

12.   Er-a svá gott
       sem gott kveða
       ǫl alda sonum.
       Því at færa veit
       er fleira drekkr,
       síns til geðs gumi.

13.   Óminnishegri heitir
       sá er yfir ǫlðrum þrumir,

9.   A man is happy
        if he finds praise and wisdom
        within himself.
        Many men have received
        bad advice
        by trusting someone else.

10.   A traveler cannot bring
        a better burden on the road
        than plenty of wisdom.
        It will prove better than money
        in an unfamiliar place—
        wisdom is the comfort of the poor.

11.   A traveler cannot bring
        a better burden on the road
        than plenty of wisdom,
        and he can bring
        no worse a burden
        than too much alcohol.

12.   There is not as much good
        as men claim there is
        in alcohol for one's well-being.
        A man knows less
        as he drinks more,
        and loses more and more of his wisdom.

13.   It's as if a memory-stealing heron
        broods overhead while you drink,

hann stelr geði guma.
Þess fugls fjǫðrum
ek fjǫtraðr var'k
í garði Gunnlaðar.

14. Ǫlr ek varð,
varð ofrǫlvi,
at ins fróða Fjalars.
Því er ǫlðr bazt
at aptr of heimtir
hverr sitt geð gumi.

15. Þagalt ok hugalt
skyli þjóðans barn,
ok vígdjarft vera.
Glaðr ok reifr
skyli gumna hverr,
unz sinn bíðr bana.

16. Ósnjallr ψ
hyggsk munu ey lifa
ef hann við víg varask,
en elli gefr
honum engi frið,
þótt honum geirar gefi.

17. Kópir afglapi
er til kynnis kømr—
þylsk hann um, eða þrumir.
Allt er senn

and steals your mind away.
I myself have been trapped
in that bird's feathers,
when I drank at Gunnlod's home.

14.   I was drunk,
      I was too drunk,
      at wise Fjalar's house.
      The best kind of feast
      is the one you go home from
      with all your wits about you.

15.   A noble man should
      be silent, thoughtful,
      and bold in battle.
      But every man should also
      be cheerful and happy,
      till the inevitable day of death.

16.   An unwise man
      thinks he'll live forever
      if only he can avoid a fight,
      but old age
      will give him no peace,
      even if weapons do.

17.   It's a fool who stares
      when he comes to a feast—
      he talks to himself, or he broods.
      As soon as

ef hann sylg um getr,
uppi er þá geð guma.

18. Sá einn veit
er víða ratar
ok hefir fjǫlð um farit
hverju geði
stýrir gumna hverr.
Sá er vitandi er vits.

19. Haldi-t ψ á keri,
drekki þó at hófi mjǫð.
Mæli þarft eða þegi.
Ókynnis þess
vár þik engi ψ
at þú gangir snemma at sofa.

20. Gráðugr halr,
nema geðs viti,
etr sér aldrtrega.
Opt fær hløgis
er með horskum kømr
manni heimskum magi.

21. Hjarðir þat vitu
nær þær heim skulu
ok ganga þá af grasi,
en ósviðr ψ
kann ævagi
síns um mál maga.

he gets a drink,
he'll say anything he knows.

18.   Only a man
who is wide-traveled
and has wandered far
can know something
about how other men think.
Such a man is wise.

19.   Don't hold on to the mead-horn,
but drink your fair share.
Say something useful or stay quiet.
And no one else
will judge you poorly
if you go to sleep early.

20.   A gluttonous man,
unless he watches himself,
will eat to his own detriment.
Wise men will often
ridicule a fool
on account of his belly.

21.   Even cows know
when they should go home
and leave behind the fields,
but an unwise man
does not know
the measure of his own appetite.

22. Vesall ψ
    ok illa skapi
    hlær at hvívetna.
    Hittki hann veit
    er hann vita þyrfti:
    at hann er-at vamma vanr.

23. Ósviðr ψ
    vakir um allar nætr
    ok hyggr at hvívetna.
    Þá er móðr
    er at morni kømr,
    allt er víl sem var.

24. Ósnotr ψ
    hyggr sér alla vera
    viðhlæjendr vini.
    Hittki hann finnr,
    þótt þeir um hann fár lesi,
    ef hann með snotrum sitr.

25. [Ósnotr ψ
    hyggr sér alla vera
    viðhlæjendr vini.]
    Þá þat finnr,
    er at þingi kømr,
    at hann á formælendr fá.

26. Ósnotr ψ
    þykkisk allt vita

22. A stupid man
    and an undisciplined one
    laughs at everything.
    He hasn't learned
    a lesson that would do him good:
    he himself isn't flawless.

23. A fool
    stays awake all night
    worrying about everything.
    He's fatigued
    when the morning comes,
    and his problems remain unsolved.

24. An unwise man
    thinks anyone who laughs with him
    is his friend.
    He doesn't understand
    that the wise are mocking him,
    even when he overhears them.

25. An unwise man
    thinks anyone who laughs with him
    is his friend,
    but he won't find these friends
    when he goes to court—
    no one will speak on his behalf.

26. A stupid man
    thinks he knows everything

ef hann á sér í vá veru.
Hittki hann veit
hvat hann skal við kveða,
ef hans freista firar.

27. Ósnotr [maðr],
er með aldir kømr,
þat er bazt at hann þegi.
Engi þat veit
at hann ekki kann,
nema hann mæli til mart.
Veit-a ψ
hinn er vætki veit
þótt hann mæli til mart.

28. Fróðr sá þykkisk
er fregna kann,
ok segja it sama.
Eyvitu leyna
megu ýta synir
því er gengr um guma.

29. Ørna mælir
sá er æva þegir
staðlausu stafi.
Hraðmælt tunga,
nema haldendr eigi,
opt sér ógott um gelr.

if he hides himself in a corner.
But he doesn't even know
what he'll answer,
if men ask him questions.

27. It's best for a fool
to keep his mouth shut
among other people.
No one will know
he knows nothing,
if he says nothing.
An ignorant man
doesn't know how little he knows,
no matter how much he talks.

28. You will seem wise
if you know the answer,
and know how to explain it.
People are not able
to keep a secret
of what they hear about other people.

29. You will say plenty of nothing
with all your talking
if you never close your mouth.
A hasty tongue,
unless it's disciplined,
often earns its owner punishment.

30. At augabragði
skal-a ψ annan hafa,
þótt til kynnis komi.
Margr þá fróðr þykkisk
ef hann freginn er-at,
ok nái hann þurrfjallr þruma.

31. Fróðr þykkisk
sá er flátta tekr
gestr at gest hæðinn.
Veit-a gǫrla
sá er um verði glissir,
þótt hann með grǫmum glami.

32. Gumnar margir
erusk gagnhollir,
en at virði rekask.
Aldar róg
þat mun æ vera:
órir gestr við gest.

33. Árliga verðar
skyli ψ opt fá,
nema til kynnis komi.
Sitr ok snópir,
lætr sem sólginn sé,
ok kann fregna at fá.

34. Afhvarf mikit
er til ills vinar,

30. No one should
    ridicule anyone else,
    even if he comes visiting.
    Many a man seems wise
    if he is never questioned,
    and he gets to brood with dry skin.

31. A man may seem wise
    if he pokes fun at another
    and disdains a fellow guest.
    But the man who talks
    behind another man's back
    knows little, even if he laughs with men.

32. Many men
    are kind to one another,
    but will fight at a feast.
    There will always
    be conflict between men:
    a guest will fight a guest.

33. You should eat
    your meals early,
    unless you're visiting a friend.
    A hungry man
    sits and gets sluggish,
    and his wits are impaired.

34. It's a long and crooked walk
    to a bad friend,

þótt á brautu búi.
En til góðs vinar
liggja gagnvegir,
þótt hann sé firr farinn.

35. Ganga [skal.]
Skal-a gestr vera
ey í einum stað.
Ljúfr verðr leiðr
ef lengi sitr
annars fletjum á.

36. Bú er betra,
þótt lítit sé—
halr er heima hverr.
Þótt tvær geitr eigi
ok taugreptan sal,
þat er þó betra en bøn.

37. [Bú er betra,
þótt lítit sé—
halr er heima hverr.]
Blóðugt er hjarta
þeim er biðja skal
sér í mál hvert matar.

38. Vápnum sínum
skal-a ψ velli á
feti ganga framarr;
því at óvíst er at vita

even if he lives nearby.
But it's an easy road
to a good friend,
no matter how long the journey.

35. You should keep moving.
You should never be a guest forever
in any one place.
Your welcome will wear out
if you stay too long
beneath another's roof.

36. It's better to have a home,
even if it's little—
everyone should call somewhere "home."
Even if you own just two goats
beneath a faulty roof,
that's still better than begging.

37. Better to have a home,
even if it's little—
everyone should call somewhere "home."
Your heart will be wounded
if you have to beg for every meal
from somebody else.

38. Never go
even a single step
without a weapon at your side;
you never know

nær verðr á vegum úti
geirs um þǫrf guma.

39. Fann'k-a ek mildan mann
eða svá matar góðan
at ei væri þiggja þegit,
eða síns fjár
svá gj[ǫflan]
at leið sé laun ef þegi.

40. Fjár síns
er fengit hefr
skyli-t ψ þǫrf þola.
Opt sparir leiðum
þat's hefir ljúfum hugat—
mart gengr verr en varir.

41. Vápnum ok váðum
skulu vinir gleðjask;
þat er á sjálfum sýnst.
Viðrgefendr ok endrgefendr
erusk lengst vinir
ef þat bíðr at verða vel.

42. Vin sínum
skal ψ vinr vera,
ok gjalda gjǫf við gjǫf.
Hlátr við hlátri
skyli hǫlðar taka,
en lausung við lygi.

when you might find yourself
in need of a spear.

39. I have never met a man so generous
    nor so hospitable
    that he would not welcome repayment,
    nor have I met a man
    so giving that he'd turn down
    a thing offered in return.

40. Do not be so sparing
    in using your money
    that you don't use it for your own needs.
    Often what you save for your children
    will end up in the hands of your enemies—
    many things will go worse than you expect.

41. Friends should provide their friends
    with weapons and clothing;
    this kind of generosity shows.
    Generous mutual giving
    is the key
    to lifelong friendship.

42. Be a friend
    to your friend,
    and repay each gift with a gift.
    Repay laughter
    with laughter,
    repay treachery with treachery.

43. Vin sínum
    skal ψ vinr vera,
    þeim ok þess vin,
    en óvinar síns
    skyli engi ψ
    vinar vinr vera.

44. Veiztu, ef þú vin átt,
    þann er þú vel trúir,
    ok vill þú af honum gott geta,
    geði skaltu við þann blanda,
    ok gjǫfum skipta,
    fara at finna opt.

45. Ef þú átt annan,
    þann's þú illa trúir,
    vildu af honum þó gott geta—
    fagrt skaltu við þann mæla,
    en flátt hyggja,
    ok gjalda lausung við lygi.

46. Þat er enn of þann,
    er þú illa trúir,
    ok þér er grunr at hans geði:
    hlæja skaltu við þeim,
    ok um hug mæla,
    glík skulu gjǫld gjǫfum.

47. Ungr var ek forðum,
    fór ek einn saman,

43.   Be a friend
      to your friend
      and also to his friend,
      but never be a friend
      to the enemy
      of your friend.

44.   If you have a good friend,
      and really trust him,
      and want good to come of your friendship,
      you should speak your mind with him,
      exchange gifts,
      visit him often.

45.   But if you have another friend,
      and you mistrust him
      but want to benefit from him, nonetheless—
      you should speak to him kindly,
      flatter him,
      and repay his treachery with your own.

46.   This same friend,
      if you mistrust him,
      and suspect him to be false in his words:
      you should talk with him,
      laugh with him,
      but repay just what he gives you.

47.   I was young once,
      I walked alone,

þá varð ek villr vega.
Auðigr þóttumsk
er ek annan fann—
ψ er manns gaman.

48. Mildir, frøknir
menn bazt lifa,
sjaldan sút ala.
En ósnjallr ψ
uggir hotvetna,
sýtir æ gløggr við gjǫfum.

49. Váðir mínar
gaf ek velli at
tveim trémǫnnum.
Rekkar þat þóttusk,
er þeir ript hǫfðu;
neiss er nøkkviðr halr.

50. Hrørnar þǫll,
sú er stendr þorpi á,
hlýr-at henni bǫrkr né barr.
Svá er ψ
sá er manngi ann;
hvat skal hann lengi lifa?

51. Eldi heitari
brennr með illum vinum
friðr fimm daga,
en þá sloknar

and I became lost on my way.
I felt like I was rich
when I met another traveler—
people's joy is in other people.

48. Kind, brave people
    live best,
    they never nurture a grudge.
    But an unwise man
    worries about everything;
    he dreads even repaying a gift.

49. I gave my clothes
    to two scarecrows,
    once when I walked in a field.
    They thought they were human
    as soon as they had clothes on;
    a naked man feels ashamed.

50. A fir-tree decays,
    standing over a farm,
    no longer protected by bark and needles.
    A person is the same way
    if nobody loves him;
    how will he live much longer?

51. The friendship
    among false friends
    burns warmly for five days,
    but then it's extinguished

er inn sétti kømr,
ok versnar allr vinskapr.

52. Mikit eitt
skal-a manni gefa;
opt kaupir sér í litlu lof.
Með hálfum hleif
ok með hǫllu keri
fekk ek mér félaga.

53. Lítilla sanda,
lítilla sæva—
lítil eru geð guma.
Því allir menn
urðu-t jafnspakir,
hálb er ǫld hvar.

54. Meðalsnotr
skyli manna hverr,
æva til snotr sé.
Þeim er fyrða
fegrst at lifa
er vel mart vitu.

55. [Meðalsnotr
skyli manna hverr,
æva til snotr sé.]
Því at snotrs manns hjarta
verðr sjaldan glatt
ef sá er alsnotr er á.

by the sixth day,
and the friendship is over.

52. You should not give
    only big gifts;
    often a little thing will win you favor.
    I have won friends
    with just half a loaf of bread
    and a bowl of soup.

53. Where the beaches are small,
    it's a small sea that washes them—
    and so it is with little minds.
    Not everyone
    is equally wise,
    but the average is moderately wise.

54. You should be
    only a little wise,
    never too wise.
    The happiest people
    throughout their lives
    are those who know just enough.

55. You should be
    only a little wise,
    never too wise.
    A wise man's heart
    is seldom glad
    if he's truly wise.

56. [Meðalsnotr
skyli manna hverr,
æva til snotr sé.]
Ørlǫg sín
viti engi ψ fyrir;
þeim er sorgalausastr sefi.

57. Brandr af brandi
brenn unz brunninn er;
funi kveykisk af funa.
ψ af manni
verðr at máli kuðr,
en til dølskr af dul.

58. Ár skal rísa,
[sá] er annars vill
fé, eða fjǫr, hafa.
Sjaldan liggjandi úlfr
lær um getr,
né sofandi ψ sigr.

59. Ár skal rísa
sá er á yrkjendr fá,
ok ganga síns verka á vit.
Mart um dvelr
þann er um morgin sefr;
hálfr er auðr und hvǫtum.

60. Þurra skíða
ok þakinna næfra,

56.   You should be
      only a little wise,
      never too wise.
      It's best not to know
      your fate beforehand;
      you'll live happier if you don't.

57.   A torch is lit by another
      and burns till it's burned out;
      a fire is kindled by another fire.
      A man becomes wise
      by speaking with other men,
      but foolish by keeping to himself.

58.   Rise early, if you want
      to take another man's
      property, or his life.
      A sleeping wolf
      seldom gets his meat,
      or a sleeping warrior a victory.

59.   Rise early
      if you have no one to work for you,
      and get straight to work.
      You lose more than time
      if you sleep when it dawns;
      for the early riser, wealth is half-won.

60.   You should know how
      to dry logs for firewood

þess kann ψ mjǫt,
ok þess viðar
er vinnask megi
mál ok misseri.

61. Þveginn ok mettr
ríði ψ þingi at,
þótt hann sé-t væddr til vel.
Skúa ok bróka
skammisk engi ψ,
né hests enn heldr,
þótt hann hafi-t góðan.

62. Snapir ok gnapir
er til sævar kømr,
ǫrn á aldinn mar.
Svá er ψ
er með mǫrgum kømr
ok á formælendr fá.

63. Fregna ok segja
skal fróðra hverr,
sá er vill heitinn horskr.
Einn vita,
né annarr skal—
þjóð veit, ef þrír'ru.

64. Ríki sitt
skyli ráðsnotra hverr
í hófi hafa.

and bark for roofing,
and also this:
the right measure of wood
for each time and season.

61. You should always go out
    well-kempt and well-fed,
    even if you can't afford good clothes.
    You should not be ashamed
    of your shoes and pants,
    nor of your horse,
    even if it's not a good one.

62. A hungry eagle snaps his beak
    and stretches out his neck,
    when the sea comes into sight.
    People get the same look about them
    when they walk among strangers
    and have no one to speak well of them.

63. If you want to be called wise,
    you should know how
    to ask and answer wisely.
    Tell your secret to one person,
    never to two—
    everyone knows, if three people know.

64. A wise man
    should use his abilities
    only in moderation.

Þá hann þat finnr,
er með frǿknum kømr,
at engi er einna hvatastr.

65. Orða þeira
er ψ ǫðrum segir
opt hann gjǫld um getr.

66. Mikilsti snemma
kom ek í marga staði,
en til síð í suma.
Ǫl var drukkit,
sumt var ólagat;
sjaldan hittir leiðr í lið.

67. Hér ok hvar
myndi mér heim of boðit,
ef þyrfta'k at málungi mat,
eða tvau lær hengi
at ins tryggva vinar
þar's ek hafða eitt etit.

68. Eldr er beztr
með ýta sonum,
ok sólar sýn—
heilyndi sitt,
ef ψ hafa náir,
án við lǫst at lifa.

Then he finds,
when he is among the bold,
that no one is bravest of all.

65. You will often
get repayment in kind
for the words you speak to others.

66. I have come too early
to some events
and too late to others.
The drinks were all gone,
or else not even made;
a hated man seldom finds the right time.

67. Now and then
I've been invited to a friend's home,
as long as I had no need for food,
or as long as I could make
my inhospitable host's cellars
fuller rather than emptier.

68. Fire is best
for mortals,
and sunshine—
and also good health,
if you have it,
and living beyond reproach.

69. Er-at ψ alls vesall,
þótt hann sé illa heill—
sumr er af sonum sæll,
sumr af frændum,
sumr af fé ørnu,
sumr af verkum vel.

70. Betra er lifðum
en sé ólifðum—
ey getr kvikr kú.
Eld sá ek upp brenna
auðgum manni fyrir,
en úti var dauðr fyr durum.

71. Haltr ríðr hrossi,
hjǫrð rekr handarvanr,
daufr vegr ok dugir.
Blindr er betri
en brenndr sé;
nýtr manngi nás.

72. Sonr er betri,
þótt sé síð of alinn,
eptir genginn guma.
Sjaldan bautarsteinar
standa brautu nær
nema reisi niðr at nið.

73. Tveir'ru eins herjar;
tunga er hǫfuðs bani.

69. No one is totally wretched,
    even if his health is bad—
    some find happiness in their children,
    some in their kin,
    some in their money,
    some in work well done.

70. Better to be alive,
    no matter what, than dead—
    only the living enjoy anything.
    I saw a fire burning
    for a rich man,
    and he lay dead outside the door.

71. A limping man can ride a horse,
    a handless man can herd,
    a deaf man can fight and win.
    It's better even to be blind
    than fuel for the funeral pyre;
    what can a dead man do?

72. Better to have a son than not,
    even if he's born late in life,
    even if he's born after you die.
    You'll rarely see memorials or graves
    standing near the road
    that were raised for men without sons.

73. Two men will defeat one;
    your tongue can endanger your head.

Er mér í heðin hvern
handar væni.

74. Nótt verðr feginn,
sá er nesti trúir,
skammar'ru skips rár.
Hverb er haustgríma.
Fjǫlð um viðrir
á fimm dǫgum,
en meira á mánaði.

75. Veit-a hinn
er vætki veit.
Margr verðr af ǫðrum api.
ψ er auðigr,
annarr óauðigr,
skyli-t þann vítka vár.

76. Deyr fé,
deyja frændr,
deyr sjálfr it sama.
En orðstírr
deyr aldregi
hveim er sér góðan getr.

77. [Deyr fé,
deyja frændr,
deyr sjálfr it sama.]
Ek veit einn

In every hand hidden by a cloak
I expect to see a weapon.

74. The seaman is glad at evening,
    looking forward to his dinner,
    and just a short distance to sail home.
    But an autumn night is untrustworthy.
    Many things can get worse
    in only five days,
    and even more in a month.

75. The ignorant man
    does not know how little he knows.
    You become foolish by listening to fools.
    One man is rich,
    another man is poor,
    neither has the other to blame.

76. Cows die,
    family die,
    you will die the same way.
    But a good reputation
    never dies
    for the one who earns it well.

77. Cows die,
    family die,
    you will die the same way.
    I know only one thing

at aldri deyr:
dómr um dauðan hvern.

78. Fullar grindr
     sá ek fyr Fitjungs sonum;
     nú bera þeir vánar vǫl.
     Svá er auðr
     sem augabragð—
     hann er valtastr vina.

79. Ósnotr ψ,
     ef eignask getr
     fé eða fljóðs munuð,
     metnaðr honum þróask
     en mannvit aldregi;
     fram gengr hann drjúgt í dul.

80. Þat er þá reynt
     er þú at rúnum spyrr,
     inum reginkunnum,
     þeim er gørðu ginnregin
     ok fáði Fimbulþulr.
     Þá hefir hann bazt ef hann þegir.

81. At kveldi skal dag leyfa,
     konu er brennd er,
     mæki er reyndr er,
     mey er gefin er,
     ís er yfir kømr,
     ǫl er drukkit er.

that never dies:
the reputation of the one who's died.

78. I saw big herds of cattle
owned by a rich man's sons;
now they carry a beggar's staff.
Wealth is like
the twinkling of an eye—
no friend could be more faithless.

79. If an unwise man
chances upon money
or a woman's love,
he will grow more arrogant
but not more intelligent;
he will be deceived about his own worth.

80. What you ask of the runes
will prove true;
they are of divine origin,
made by the mighty gods
and painted by Óðin.
You'll learn best with your mouth shut.

81. Don't praise the day until it's night,
don't praise your wife until she's burned,
don't praise the sword till after the fight,
nor your daughter till she's married,
don't praise the ice until it's crossed,
nor the ale until it's drunk.

82. Í vindi skal við hǫggva,
     veðri á sjó róa,
     myrkri við man spjalla,
     (mǫrg eru dags augu).
     Á skip skal skriðar orka,
     en á skjǫld til hlífar,
     mæki hǫggs,
     en mey til kossa.

83. Við eld skal ǫl drekka,
     en á ísi skríða,
     magran mar kaupa
     en mæki saurgan.
     Heima hest feita,
     en hund á búi.

84. Meyjar orðum
     skyli manngi trúa
     né því er kveðr kona.
     Því at á hverfanda hvéli
     váru þeim hjǫrtu skǫpuð,
     brigð í brjóst um lagið.

85. Brestanda boga,
     brennanda loga,
     gínanda úlfi,
     galandi kráku,
     rýtanda svíni,
     rótlausum viði,

82. Chop wood when the wind blows,
     row your boat on a calm sea,
     court a lover at nighttime
     (for the day has many eyes).
     Value a ship for its speed,
     a shield for its protection,
     a sword for its sharpness,
     and a woman for her kiss.

83. Drink ale by the fire,
     skate on the ice,
     buy a thin horse
     and a rusty sword.
     Give your horse food,
     and let your dog feed itself.

84. No man should trust
     the words of a girl,
     nor anything a woman says.
     Women's hearts are molded
     on a wobbly wheel.
     Faithlessness is planted at their core.

85. A breaking bow,
     a burning fire,
     a howling wolf,
     a cawing crow,
     a grunting pig,
     a rootless tree,

vaxanda vági,
vellanda katli,

86. fljúganda fleini,
fallandi báru,
ísi einnættum,
ormi hringlegnum,
brúðar beðmálum
eða brotnu sverði,
bjarnar leiki,
eða barni konungs,

87. sjúkum kálfi,
sjálfráða þræli,
vǫlu vilmæli,
val nýfelldum,

(89). bróðurbana sínum
(þótt á brautu mǿti),
húsi hálfbrunnu,
hesti alskjótum
(þá er jór ónýtr
ef einn fótr brotnar)—
verði-t ψ svá tryggr
at þessu trúi ǫllu.

(88). Akri ársánum
trúi engi ψ,
né til snemma syni—
veðr ræðr akri

a swelling wave,
a boiling kettle,

86. a flying spear,
a crashing wave,
one-night-old ice,
a coiled snake,
the words of a bride in bed,
a broken sword,
a playful bear,
the child of a king,

87. a sick calf,
a stubborn servant,
a prophet who foresees good things,
a corpse on the battlefield,

(89). your brother's killer
(even if you meet him in public),
a half-burned house,
a horse that's too fast
(remember, a horse is unusable
if only one foot breaks)—
may you never be so trusting
that you trust all these things.

(88). Do not put too much trust
in your newly planted crops,
nor in your child too early—
weather will shape the field

en vit syni,
hætt er þeira hvárt.

90. Svá er friðr kvenna
þeira er flátt hyggja,
sem aki jó óbryddum,
á ísi hálum,
teitum, tvévetrum,
ok sé tamr illa,
eða í byr óðum
beiti stjórnlausu,
eða skyli haltr henda
hrein í þáfjalli.

91. Bert ek nú mæli,
því at ek bæði veit:
brigðr er karla hugr konum.
Þá vér fegrst mælum
er vér flást hyggjum,
þat tælir horska hugi.

92. Fagrt skal mæla
ok fé bjóða
sá er vill fljóðs ást fá.
Líki leyfa
ins ljósa mans;
sá fær er frjár.

93. Ástar firna
skyli engi ψ

and whim will shape the child,
and neither will stay the same.

90.   This is the love
of deceitful women,
it is like driving an unshod horse,
a playful, young,
poorly tamed foal,
across slippery ice,
or like sailing a ship
in a wild wind,
or limping after a reindeer
after the mountains thaw.

91.   I'll speak plainly now, since
I know both men and women:
men lie to women.
We speak most eloquently
when we tell the biggest lies,
and seduce even wise women with lies.

92.   A man should speak eloquently
and offer gifts
to a woman whose love he wants.
Praise the body
of a beautiful woman;
it's the enamored man who'll win her.

93.   No man
should mock another

annan aldregi.
Opt fá á horskan
er á heimskan né fá,
lostfagrir litir.

94. Eyvitar firna
    er ψ annan skal
    þess er um margan gengr guma;
    heimska ór horskum
    gørir hǫlða sonu
    sá inn mátki munr.

95. Hugr einn þat veit
    er býr hjarta nær,
    einn er hann sér um sefa;
    engi er sótt verri
    hveim snotrum manni
    en sér engu at una.

96. Þat ek þá reynda
    er ek í reyri sat
    ok vætta'k míns munar.
    Hold ok hjarta
    var mér in horska mær,
    þeygi ek hana at heldr hefi'k.

97. Billings mey
    ek fann beðjum á,
    sólhvíta sofa.
    Jarls ynði

for falling in love.
A woman's beauty
often strikes harder
on a wise man than a fool.

94. No man
should mock another
for falling in love;
love is strong enough
to make a fool
out of a man who once was wise.

95. Only you know
what dwells in your heart
when you are alone;
but nothing is worse
for a wise person
than to have nothing to love.

96. I experienced this
when I waited among the reeds
and hoped in vain for my lover.
That wise girl
was my flesh and my heart,
though I could not call her my own.

97. I found Billing's daughter,
fair as a sun-ray,
asleep on her bed.
The life of a lord

þótti mér ekki vera
nema við þat lík at lifa.

98. "Auk nær aptni
skaltu, Óðinn, koma,
ef þú vilt þér mæla man—
allt eru óskǫp
nema ein vitim
slíkan lǫst saman."

99. Aptr ek hvarf,
ok unna þóttumsk
vísum vilja frá.
Hitt ek hugða
at ek hafa mynda
geð hennar allt ok gaman.

100. Svá kom ek næst,
at in nýta var
vígdrótt ǫll um vakin.
Með brennandum ljósum
ok bornum viði,
svá var mér vílstígr of vitaðr.

101. Ok nær morni,
er ek var enn um kominn,
þá var saldrótt um sofin—
grey eitt ek þá fann
innar góðu konu
bundit beðjum á.

seemed as nothing to me
unless I could live next to that body.

98. "You should come back
in the evening, Óðin," she said,
"if you want to woo me—
it is improper
unless we alone know
of such a scandal."

99. I turned back,
away from my wise desire,
and thought I'd already won her.
I imagined
that I would have
the woman's love and all her joy.

100. But when I came back that night,
there was a good company of warriors
awake and ready for me.
With burning flames
and torches held high,
I was shown my miserable way out.

101. And when morning came,
and I returned,
everyone in the hall was sleeping—
and then I found a watchdog
tied to the bed
of that good woman.

102. Morg er góð mær,
     ef gorva kannar,
     hugbrigð við hali;
     þá ek þat reynda
     er it ráðspaka
     teygða ek á flærðir fljóð.
     Háðungar hverrar
     leitaði mér it horska man,
     ok hafða ek þess vætki vífs.

103. Heima glaðr gumi,
     ok við gesti reifr,
     sviðr skal um sik vera.
     Minnigr ok málugr,
     ef hann vill margfróðr vera,
     opt skal góðs geta.
     Fimbulfambi heitir
     sá er fátt kann segja—
     þat er ósnotrs aðal.

104. Inn aldna jotun ek sótta,
     nú em ek aptr um kominn.
     Fátt gat ek þegjandi þar.
     Morgum orðum
     mælta ek í minn frama
     í Suttungs solum.

105. Gunnloð mér um gaf
     gullnum stóli á
     drykk ins dýra mjaðar.

102. There's many a good woman,
     if you get to know her,
     who'll change her mind about a man;
     I learned that
     when I tried
     to seduce a wise woman.
     That wise lady
     showed me every kind of shame,
     and I gained no wife for my trouble.

103. If you want to be very wise,
     be happy at home,
     and cheerful with guests.
     Cultivate wisdom,
     a good memory, and eloquence,
     and speak kind words often.
     You'll be called a fool
     if you can't say much—
     that's the mark of the unwise.

104. I visited an old giant,
     and now I've returned.
     I didn't stay silent there.
     I spoke many words
     in support of my cause
     at Suttung's hall.

105. Gunnlod, his daughter,
     gave me a drink of his precious mead
     while I sat on a golden chair.

Ill iðgjǫld
lét ek hana eptir hafa
síns ins heila hugar,
síns ins svára sefa.

106. Rata munn
létumk rúms um fá,
ok um grjót gnaga.
Yfir ok undir
stóðumk jǫtna vegir.
Svá hætta ek hǫfði til.

107. Vel keypts litar
hefi ek vel notit;
fás er fróðum vant.
Því at Óðrerir
er nú upp kominn
á alda vés jaðar.

108. Ifi er mér á
at ek væra enn kominn
jǫtna gǫrðum ór
ef ek Gunnlaðar né nyta'k,
innar góðu konu
þeirar er lǫgðum'k arm yfir.

109. Ins hindra dags
gengu hrímþursar
Háva ráðs at fregna
Háva hǫllu í;

I would later give her
a bad repayment
for her trusting mind,
for her troubled mind.

106. Giants' dwellings were
over and under me.
I used Rati's tusk
to burrow out
and gnaw away the rock—
in this way, I risked my head.

107. I made good use
of the disguise I used;
few things are too difficult for the wise.
Now Óðrerir
has come up
onto the rim of Miðgarð.

108. I doubt
I could have escaped
Jotunheim
if I hadn't used Gunnloð,
the good woman
who rested in my arms.

109. The next day
the frost-giants came
to ask Óðin's advice
in Óðin's hall;

at Bǫlverki þeir spurðu,
ef hann væri með bǫndum kominn,
eða hefði honum Suttungr of sóit.

110. Baugeið Óðinn
hygg ek at unnit hafi—
hvat skal hans tryggðum trúa?
Suttung svikinn
hann lét sumbli frá,
ok grøtta Gunnlǫðu.

111. M ál er at þylja
        þular stóli á
Urðar brunni at.
Sá ek ok þagða'k,
sá ek ok hugða'k,
hlýdda ek á manna mál.
Of rúnar heyrða ek døma,
né um ráðum þǫgðu
Háva hǫllu at,
Háva hǫllu í,
heyrða ek segja svá:

112. Ráðum'k þér, Loddfáfnir,
at þú ráð nemir,
njóta mundu ef þú nemr,
þér munu góð ef þú getr:
Nótt þú rís-at,

they inquired about that "Evildoer,"
whether he was among the gods,
or whether Suttung had killed him.

110. I believe that Óđin
swore an oath to them—
but who can trust Óđin?
He left Suttung deceived
after the banquet,
and he left Gunnlođ weeping.

111. It is time to speak
on the wise man's chair
at Urđ's well.
I saw and was silent,
I saw and I thought,
I listened to men's speech.
I heard about runes,
they were not silent with counsel
at Óđin's hall,
in Óđin's hall,
I heard them say so:

112. I counsel you, Loddfáfnir,
if you'll take my advice,
you'll profit if you learn it,
it'll do you good if you remember it:
Do not rise at night,

nema á njósn sér,
eða þú leitir þér innan út staðar.

113. Ráðum'k þér, [Loddfáfnir,
at þú ráð nemir,
njóta mundu ef þú nemr,
þér munu góð ef þú getr:]
Fjǫlkunnigri konu
skal-at-tu í faðmi sofa,
svá at hon lyki þik liðum.

114. Hon svá gørir
at þú gáir eigi
þings né þjóðans máls;
mat þú vill-at
né mannskis gaman,
ferr þú sorgafullr at sofa.

115. Ráðum'k þér, [Loddfáfnir,
at þú ráð nemir,
njóta mundu ef þú nemr,
þér munu góð ef þú getr:]
Annars konu
teygðu þér aldregi
eyrarúnu at.

116. Ráðum'k þér, [Loddfáfnir,
at þú ráð nemir,
njóta mundu ef þú nemr,
þér munu góð ef þú getr:]

unless you're spying on your enemies,
or seeking a place to relieve yourself.

113. I counsel you, Loddfáfnir,
      if you'll take my advice,
      you'll profit if you learn it,
      it'll do you good if you remember it:
      Do not sleep in the arms
      of a sorceress,
      or else she will lock your limbs.

114. She will enchant you
      so that you won't care
      for advice nor a powerful man's words;
      you will want neither food
      nor the pleasure of friends' company,
      and you will sleep full of sorrow.

115. I counsel you, Loddfáfnir,
      if you'll take my advice,
      you'll profit if you learn it,
      it'll do you good if you remember it:
      Never seduce
      another man's woman
      with whispers in her ear.

116. I counsel you, Loddfáfnir,
      if you'll take my advice,
      you'll profit if you learn it,
      it'll do you good if you remember it:

Á fjalli eða firði
ef þik fara tíðir,
fásktu at virði vel.

117. Ráðum'k þér, [Loddfáfnir,
at þú ráð nemir,
njóta mundu ef þú nemr,
þér munu góð ef þú getr:]
Illan mann
láttu aldregi
óhǫpp at þér vita,
því at af illum manni
fær þú aldregi
gjǫld ins góða hugar.

118. Ofarla bíta
ek sá einum hal
orð illrar konu—
fláráð tunga
varð honum at fjǫrlagi,
ok þeygi um sanna sǫk.

119. Ráðum'k þér, [Loddfáfnir,
at þú ráð nemir,
njóta mundu ef þú nemr,
þér munu góð ef þú getr:]
Veiztu, ef þú vin átt,
þann's þú vel trúir,
farðu at finna opt.
Því at hrísi vex

If you spend time wandering
by land or by sea,
bring plentiful provisions.

117. I counsel you, Loddfáfnir,
if you'll take my advice,
you'll profit if you learn it,
it'll do you good if you remember it:
Never let
a bad man
know of your misfortune,
for you will never
profit at all
from your good will toward a bad man.

118. I saw
a bad woman's words
bite a man in the neck—
a lying tongue
was his death,
and not even with good cause.

119. I counsel you, Loddfáfnir,
if you'll take my advice,
you'll profit if you learn it,
it'll do you good if you remember it:
If you have a friend,
and you trust him,
go and visit him often.
Weeds and high grass

ok hávu grasi
vegr er vætki trøðr.

120. Ráðum'k þér, [Loddfáfnir,
at þú ráð nemir,
njóta mundu ef þú nemr,
þér munu góð ef þú getr:]
Góðan mann
teygðu þér at gamanrúnum,
ok nem líknargaldr meðan þú lifir.

121. Ráðum'k þér, [Loddfáfnir,
at þú ráð nemir,
njóta mundu ef þú nemr,
þér munu góð ef þú getr:]
Vin þínum
ver þú aldregi
fyrri at flaumslitum.
Sorg etr hjarta
ef þú segja né náir
einhverjum allan hug.

122. Ráðum'k þér, [Loddfáfnir,
at þú ráð nemir,
njóta mundu ef þú nemr,
þér munu góð ef þú getr:]
Orðum skipta
þú skalt aldregi
við ósvinna apa.

will grow on a path
that nobody travels.

120. I counsel you, Loddfáfnir,
      if you'll take my advice,
      you'll profit if you learn it,
      it'll do you good if you remember it:
      Get a good man
      to join you in joyful talk,
      and learn a healing spell while you live.

121. I counsel you, Loddfáfnir,
      if you'll take my advice,
      you'll profit if you learn it,
      it'll do you good if you remember it:
      Never be
      the first to break
      friendship with your friend.
      Sadness will eat up your heart
      if you have no one
      you can talk to.

122. I counsel you, Loddfáfnir,
      if you'll take my advice,
      you'll profit if you learn it,
      it'll do you good if you remember it:
      You should never
      exchange words
      with someone who won't see reason.

123. Því at af illum manni
mundu aldregi
góðs laun um geta,
en góðr ψ
mun þik gørva mega
líknfastan at lofi.

124. Sifjum er þá blandat,
hverr er segja ræðr
einum allan hug.
Allt er betra
en sé brigðum at vera:
er-a sá vinr ǫðrum er vilt eitt segir.

125. Ráðum'k þér, [Loddfáfnir,
at þú ráð nemir,
njóta mundu ef þú nemr,
þér munu góð ef þú getr:]
Þrimr orðum senna
skal-at-tu þér við verra mann.
Opt inn betri bilar
þá er inn verri vegr.

126. Ráðum'k þér, [Loddfáfnir,
at þú ráð nemir,
njóta mundu ef þú nemr,
þér munu góð ef þú getr:]
Skósmiðr þú verir,
né skeptismiðr,
nema þú sjálfum þér sér;

123. You will never
     get a reward for dealing
     with a bad man,
     but a good man
     will make you well-regarded
     with his praise.

124. Men become friends
     when they can share
     their minds with one another.
     Anything is better
     than the company of liars:
     a real friend will disagree with you openly.

125. I counsel you, Loddfáfnir,
     if you'll take my advice,
     you'll profit if you learn it,
     it'll do you good if you remember it:
     Don't speak even three words
     with a man worse than you.
     Often the better man will lose
     when a worse man fights him.

126. I counsel you, Loddfáfnir,
     if you'll take my advice,
     you'll profit if you learn it,
     it'll do you good if you remember it:
     Don't make shoes,
     and don't make weapons,
     except for yourself;

skór er skapaðr illa,
eða skapt sé rangt,
þá er þér bǫls beðit.

127. Ráðum'k þér, [Loddfáfnir,
at þú ráð nemir,
njóta mundu ef þú nemr,
þér munu góð ef þú getr:]
Hvar's þú bǫl kannt,
kveðu þat bǫlvi at,
ok gef-at þínum fjándum frið.

128. Ráðum'k þér, [Loddfáfnir,
at þú ráð nemir,
njóta mundu ef þú nemr,
þér munu góð ef þú getr:]
Illu feginn
verðu aldregi,
en lát þér at góðu getit.

129. Ráðum'k þér, [Loddfáfnir,
at þú ráð nemir,
njóta mundu ef þú nemr,
þér munu góð ef þú getr:]
Upp líta
skal-at-tu í orrustu—
gjalti glíkir
verða gumna synir—
síðr þitt um heilli halir.

if there's a flaw in the shoe,
or the spearshaft is crooked,
your name will be cursed.

127. I counsel you, Loddfáfnir,
if you'll take my advice,
you'll profit if you learn it,
it'll do you good if you remember it:
When you recognize evil,
call it evil,
and give your enemies no peace.

128. I counsel you, Loddfáfnir,
if you'll take my advice,
you'll profit if you learn it,
it'll do you good if you remember it:
Never be glad
to hear bad news,
but be cheerful about good news.

129. I counsel you, Loddfáfnir,
if you'll take my advice,
you'll profit if you learn it,
it'll do you good if you remember it:
You should never look up
when you're in a fight—
men who do so
may go mad with panic—
beware, or someone may curse you.

130. Ráðum'k þér, [Loddfáfnir,
     at þú ráð nemir,
     njóta mundu ef þú nemr,
     þér munu góð ef þú getr:]
     Ef þú vilt þér góða konu
     kveðja at gamanrúnum,
     ok fá fǫgnuð af,
     fǫgru skaltu heita,
     ok láta fast vera,
     leiðisk manngi gott ef getr.

131. Ráðum'k þér, [Loddfáfnir,
     at þú ráð nemir,
     njóta mundu ef þú nemr,
     þér munu góð ef þú getr:]
     Varan bið ek þik vera,
     ok eigi ofvaran:
     ver þú við ǫl varastr,
     ok við annars konu,
     ok við þat it þriðja:
     at þjófar né leiki.

132. Ráðum'k þér, [Loddfáfnir,
     at þú ráð nemir,
     njóta mundu ef þú nemr,
     þér munu góð ef þú getr:]
     At háði né hlátri
     hafðu aldregi
     gest né ganganda.

130. I counsel you, Loddfáfnir,
     if you'll take my advice,
     you'll profit if you learn it,
     it'll do you good if you remember it:
     If you want to win a good woman
     with joyful talk,
     and you want to enjoy her—
     make promises to her,
     and keep your promises,
     you'll never regret winning such a prize.

131. I counsel you, Loddfáfnir,
     if you'll take my advice,
     you'll profit if you learn it,
     it'll do you good if you remember it:
     I advise you to be wary,
     though never fearful:
     be most wary about drinking,
     about other men's women,
     and about a third thing:
     about men and their temptation to steal.

132. I counsel you, Loddfáfnir,
     if you'll take my advice,
     you'll profit if you learn it,
     it'll do you good if you remember it:
     Never mock,
     never laugh at,
     a guest nor a wanderer.

133. Opt vitu ógǫrla
þeir er sitja inni fyrir
hvers þeir'ru kyns er koma,
er-at ψ svá góðr
at galli né fylgi,
né svá illr at einugi dugi.

134. Ráðum'k þér, [Loddfáfnir,
at þú ráð nemir,
njóta mundu ef þú nemr,
þér munu góð ef þú getr:]
At hárum þul
hlæðu aldregi.
Opt er gott þat er gamlir kveða;
opt ór skǫrpum belg
skilin orð koma.
Þeim er hangir með hám,
ok skollir með skrám,
ok váfir með vílmǫgum.

135. Ráðum'k þér, [Loddfáfnir,
at þú ráð nemir,
njóta mundu ef þú nemr,
þér munu góð ef þú getr:]
Gest þú né gey-a
né á grind hrækir—
get þú váluðum vel.

136. Rammt er þat tré,
er ríða skal

133. Those inside the house
     rarely know anything
     about the stranger who knocks at their door,
     but there is no man so good
     that he has no flaw,
     nor a man so bad he's good for nothing.

134. I counsel you, Loddfáfnir,
     if you'll take my advice,
     you'll profit if you learn it,
     it'll do you good if you remember it:
     Never laugh
     at an old man.
     There is often wisdom in what old men say;
     wise words will often
     come from a gray-bearded mouth.
     From the one who hangs with dried skins,
     who swings with dried skins,
     who waves with despicable men.

135. I counsel you, Loddfáfnir,
     if you'll take my advice,
     you'll profit if you learn it,
     it'll do you good if you remember it:
     Never spite a guest
     nor spit at his entrance—
     treat a poor wanderer well.

136. It's a strong door
     that ought to open

ǫllum at upploki.
Baug þú gef,
eða þat biðja mun
þér læs hvers á liðu.

137. Ráðum'k þér, [Loddfáfnir,
at þú ráð nemir,
njóta mundu ef þú nemr,
þér munu góð ef þú getr:]
Hvar's þú ǫl drekkir,
kjós þú þér jarðar megin,
því at jǫrð tekr við ǫlðri,
en eldr við sóttum,
eik við abbindi,
ax við fjǫlkynngi,
hǫll við hýrógi,
(heiptum skal mána kveðja),
beiti við bitsóttum,
en við bǫlvi rúnar,
fold skal við flóði taka.

138. Veit ek at ek hekk
vindga meiði á
nætr allar níu,
geiri undaðr
ok gefinn Óðni,
sjálfr sjálfum mér,
á þeim meiði

to let everyone in.
Give a visitor something,
or he will call
every curse down on your limbs.

137. I counsel you, Loddfáfnir,
if you'll take my advice,
you'll profit if you learn it,
it'll do you good if you remember it:
When you drink beer,
choose the might of the earth,
for the earth is good against beer,
and fire against sickness,
oak against an irritable bowel,
wheat against magic,
an elder-tree against family quarrels,
maggots against venomous bites,
runes against evil,
ground against water.
Swear your hate beneath the moon.

138. I know that I hung
on a wind-battered tree
nine long nights,
pierced by a spear
and given to Óðin,
myself to myself,
on that tree

er manngi veit
hvar's hann af rótum renn.

139. Við hleifi mik søldu,
né við hornigi.
Nýsta ek niðr,
nam ek upp rúnar—
øpandi nam—
fell ek aptr þaðan.

140. Fimbulljóð níu
nam ek af inum frægja syni
Bǫlþórs, Bestlu fǫður,
ok ek drykk of gat
ins dýra mjaðar,
ausinn Óðreri.

141. Þá nam ek frævask,
ok fróðr vera,
ok vaxa ok vel hafask.
Orð mér af orði
orðs leitaði,
verk mér af verki
verks leitaði.

142. Rúnar munt þú finna,
ok ráðna stafi,
mjǫk stóra stafi,
mjǫk stinna stafi,
er fáði Fimbulþulr,

whose roots grow in a place
no one has ever seen.

139. No one gave me food,
no one gave me drink.
At the end I peered down,
I took the runes—
screaming, I took them—
and then I fell.

140. I learned nine spells
from the famous son of Bolthór,
the father of Bestla,
and I won a drink
of that precious mead,
poured from Óđrerir.

141. I began to be fruitful,
I became wise,
I grew, and I thrived.
One word chased another word
flowing from my mouth,
one deed chased another deed
flowing from my hands.

142. You will find runes,
runic letters to read,
very great runes,
very powerful runes,
which Óđin painted,

ok gørðu ginnregin,
ok reist Hróptr rǫgna.

143. Óðinn með ásum,
en fyr álfum Dáinn,
ok Dvalinn dvergum fyrir,
Ásviðr jǫtnum fyrir,
ek reist sjálfr sumar.

144. Veiztu hvé rísta skal?
Veiztu hvé ráða skal?
Veiztu hvé fá skal?
Veiztu hvé freista skal?
Veiztu hvé biðja skal?
Veiztu hvé blóta skal?
Veiztu hvé senda skal?
Veiztu hvé sóa skal?

145. Betra er óbeðit
en sé ofblótit;
ey sér til gildis gjǫf.
Betra er ósent
en sé ofsóit.
Svá Þundr um reist
fyr þjóða rǫk,
þar hann upp um reis
er hann aptr of kom.

146. Ljóð ek þau kann
er kann-at þjóðans kona

and which the holy gods made,
and which Óðin carved.

143. Óðin carved for the gods,
and Dáin for the elves,
Dvalin for the dwarves,
and Ásviđ for the giants;
I carved some myself.

144. Do you know how to write them?
Do you know how to read them?
Do you know how to paint them?
Do you know how to test them?
Do you know how to ask them?
Do you know how to bless them?
Do you know how to send them?
Do you know how to offer them?

145. It is better not to pray at all
than to pray for too much;
nothing will be given that you won't repay.
It is better to sacrifice nothing
than to offer too much.
Óðin carved this
before the birth of humankind,
when he rose up
and returned again.

146. I know magic spells
that no woman knows

ok mannskis mǫgr.
'Hjálp' heitir eitt,
en þat þér hjálpa mun
við sǫkum ok sorgum,
ok sútum gǫrvǫllum.

147. Þat kann ek annat,
er þurfu ýta synir
þeir er vilja læknar lifa.

148. Þat kann ek þriðja;
ef mér verðr þǫrf mikil
hapts við mína heiptmǫgu,
eggjar ek deyfi
minna andskota,
bíta-t þeim vápn né velir.

149. Þat kann ek it fjórða;
ef mér fyrðar bera
bǫnd at bóglimum,
svá ek gel
at ek ganga má.
Sprettr mér af fótum fjǫturr,
en af hǫndum hapt.

150. Þat kann ek it fimmta;
ef ek sé af fári skotinn
flein í fólki vaða,
flýgr-a hann svá stinnt

and no man, either.
The first is called "Help,"
and it will help you
in lawsuits and sadness,
and all kinds of worries.

147. I know a second spell
which men need
if they want to heal others.

148. I know a third spell;
if I have a great need
to thwart my enemies,
I dull the edges
of their weapons,
and none of their blades will bite.

149. I know a fourth spell;
if chains and locks are placed
upon my limbs,
I cast this spell
so that I can escape.
The chains burst from my hands,
the locks burst from my feet.

150. I know a fifth spell;
if I see a spear cast
into a crowd of battling foes,
it cannot fly so fast

at ek stǫðvi'g-a'k,
ef ek hann sjónum of sé'k.

151. Þat kann ek it sétta;
ef mik særir þegn
á rótum rás viðar,
ok þann hal
er mik heipta kveðr,
þann eta mein heldr en mik.

152. Þat kann ek it sjaunda;
ef ek sé hávan loga
sal um sessmǫgum,
brennr-at svá breitt
at ek honum bjargi'g-a'k;
þann kann ek galdr at gala.

153. Þat kann ek it átta;
er ǫllum er
nytsamligt at nema.
Hvar's hatr vex
með hildings sonum,
þat má ek bǿta brátt.

154. Þat kann ek it níunda;
ef mik nauðr um stendr
at bjarga fari mínu á floti,
vind ek kyrri
vági á
ok svæfi'k allan sæ.

that I can't stop its flight,
as long as I can see it.

151. I know a sixth spell;
if a man carves a curse against me
in the roots of a gnarled tree,
I call this spell down
upon that man,
and his curse harms him instead of me.

152. I know a seventh spell;
if I see a great flame
consuming a hall full of people,
it cannot burn so bright
that I cannot save those inside;
I know how to cast this spell.

153. I know an eighth spell;
it would be useful
for anyone to learn it.
When hate arises
between any two people,
I can cool their tempers.

154. I know a ninth spell;
if the need arises
for me to save a ship upon the sea,
I can calm the wind
upon the waves
and soothe the sea to sleep.

155. Þat kann ek it tíunda;
ef ek sé túnriður
leika lopti á,
ek svá vinn'k
at þær villar fara,
sinna heimhama,
sinna heimhuga.

156. Þat kann ek it ellipta;
ef ek skal til orrustu
leiða langvini,
undir randir ek gel
en þeir með ríki fara;
heilir hildar til,
heilir hildi frá.
Koma þeir heilir hvaðan.

157. Þat kann ek it tólpta;
ef ek sé, á tré uppi,
váfa virgilná,
svá ek ríst
ok í rúnum fá'k,
at sá gengr gumi
ok mælir við mik.

158. Þat kann ek it þrettánda;
ef ek skal þegn ungan
verpa vatni á,
mun-at hann falla

155. I know a tenth spell;
     if I see witches
     at play in the air,
     I can cast this spell
     so that they get lost,
     so they can't find their skins,
     so they can't find their minds.

156. I know an eleventh spell;
     if I lead old friends
     into a battle,
     I enchant their shields
     so that they will have the victory;
     they will go to battle unharmed,
     and return from battle unharmed.
     They will come home without harm.

157. I know a twelfth spell;
     if I see, hanging from a tree,
     a dead man's corpse,
     I carve some runes
     and paint them,
     and then that corpse will walk
     and speak with me.

158. I know a thirteenth spell;
     if I throw water
     upon a young man,
     he will never be killed

þótt hann í fólk komi;
hnígr-a sá halr fyr hjǫrum.

159. Þat kann ek it fjórtánda;
ef ek skal fyrða liði
telja tíva fyrir.
Ása ok álfa
ek kann allra skil,
fár kann ósnotr svá.

160. Þat kann ek it fimmtánda;
er gól Þjóðreyrir
dvergr fyr Dellings durum.
Afl gól hann ásum,
en álfum frama,
hyggju Hróptatý.

161. Þat kann ek it sextánda;
ef ek vil ins svinna mans
hafa geð allt ok gaman,
hugi ek hverfi
hvítarmri konu
ok sný ek hennar ǫllum sefa.

162. Þat kann ek it sjautjánda,
at mik mun seint firrask
it manunga man.
Ljóða þessa
munðu, Loddfáfnir,
lengi vanr vera.

even if he goes into battle;
that man will not die from violence.

159. I know a fourteenth spell;
it allows me to count
all the gods for men.
I know the names
of all the gods and elves,
and few who are fools can say that.

160. I know a fifteenth spell;
the dwarf Thjóðreyrir
cast it before Delling's doors.
He conjured power for the gods,
courage for the elves,
and knowledge for Óðin.

161. I know a sixteenth spell;
if I want to win over a cunning woman
and have her all to myself,
I can change the mind
of that lovely-armed beauty
and win her favor for myself.

162. I know a seventeenth spell,
to prevent a beautiful woman
from shunning me.
You'll go without
these spells, Loddfáfnir,
for a long time.

Þó sé þér góð ef þú getr,
nýt ef þú nemr,
þǫrf ef þú þiggr.

163. Þat kann ek it átjánda
er ek æva kenni'k
mey né manns konu—
allt er betra,
er einn um kann,
þat fylgir ljóða lokum—
nema þeiri einni
er mik armi verr,
eða mín systir sé.

164. Nú eru Háva mál kveðin
Háva hǫllu í,
allþǫrf ýta sonum,
óþǫrf jǫtna sonum;
heill sá er kvað,
heill sá er kann,
njóti sá er nam,
heilir þeir's hlýddu.

But they'd profit you if you learned them,
they'd do you good if you remembered them,
they'd suit your needs if you could use them.

163. I know an eighteenth spell
     which I will never teach
     to a girl or a woman,
     unless maybe to the one
     I embrace in sleep,
     or my sister.
     It is much better
     that one alone should know this,
     which is the last of the spells.

164. Now the words of the One-Eyed
     are heard in Óðin's hall,
     for the benefit of humans,
     for the harm of giants;
     health to you who speak them,
     health to you who know them,
     profit to you who learn them,
     health to you who hear them.

Commentary on the Old Norse Text of *Hávamál*

The Old Norse text of *Hávamál* presented in this volume is based on my own reading of the manuscript itself, the *Codex Regius*, catalogued as GKS 2365 4to at the Árni Magnússon Institute in Reykjavík, Iceland. I examined the manuscript closely in person during the summer of 2007, and again in winter 2018–19 in high-quality scans provided by the Institute.

Stanza numbers, and divisions into lines, are not found in the manuscript, but are based on common agreement among modern scholars. Naturally, there is minor variation among editions and translations, but in the twentieth and twenty-first centuries scholars have generally been reluctant to rearrange the text in any dramatic way. Previous generations of scholars, however, and some modern enthusiasts, have often numbered the stanzas very differently or rearranged them entirely, so some caution must be applied in comparing editions. Note also that many editors and translators, especially outside Scandinavia, consider the lines of Old Norse poetry only "half-lines," and print them accordingly, so that a stanza that I print with eight lines will appear with four in many such editions.

Old Norse manuscripts have little in the way of capitalization and punctuation, and no consistent system of either, thus I have punctuated and capitalized the Old Norse text in a manner consistent with the standards of present-day English. I have written vowels as short or long in accordance with "classical" Old Norse orthography; where modern scholars are uncertain of the length of a vowel I have made my best guess based on the word's etymology or on related words in present-day Scandinavian dialects. As most other editors have done, I have also "silently" expanded Old Norse manuscript abbreviations and shorthand symbols, so that for instance *hō* is written out as the full word *hon* "she," *h* as *hann* "he," the Tironian nota (a symbol similar in shape to the number *7*) as the full word *ok* "and," etc.

The reader of *Hávamál* will notice that multiple stanzas may reuse the same first half. In the manuscript, after the first occurrence of such a repeated formula, the second and later occurrences will generally be abbreviated. For example, the first half of stanza 10 is *Byrði betri / berr-at ψ brautu at / en sé mannvit mikit*. In stanza 11, the same first half is repeated, but this is indicated in the manuscript simply by abbreviating these three lines to *Byrði b.b.* In the same way, stanza 112 opens with the formula *Ráðum'k þér, Loddfáfnir, / at þú ráð nemir, / njóta mundu ef þú nemr, / þér munu góð ef þú getr*. This is plainly intended to be reused in almost every other stanza through stanza 137, but in most of them these four lines are abbreviated to simply *Ráðum'k þ'* (with ' here representing a comma-like mark made over the letter *þ* to indicate that it stands for the word *þér* "you"). Where I have filled in one stanza with lines repeated from another stanza in this way, I have enclosed the lines that have been filled in with square brackets [ ]. I have also enclosed words or parts of words in square brackets if they must be supplied for other reasons, such as simple scribal error, as with *[maðr]* in the first line of stanza 27, or *gj[ǫflan]* in the fifth line of stanza 39.

In numerous stanzas (e.g., 50, 62, 75), the word *maðr* "man/person," or an inflected form of it, is rendered by the scribe of the

Codex Regius with the Younger Futhark rune that represents the consonant [m], named *maðr* "man/person." This runic letter as used in the manuscript is almost identical in form to a minuscule Greek letter *ψ* "psi," and so I have rendered it as such rather than with the Unicode version of the runic letter (ᛘ). The letter is to be read as the word *maðr*. For examples of the rune as used in the manuscript, see the sample page from the *Codex Regius* (page 04r) reproduced before the Introduction to this volume; the first occurrence on that page is in line 11 (which is st. 38, line 2). Where the word *maðr* is instead spelled out in the manuscript (as in line 2 of st. 6), I have spelled it out as well.

I have separated the negative suffix *a*, *t*, or *at* from the preceding word by use of a hyphen; e.g., *er-a* or *er-at* "is not," *veit-a* "doesn't know," *skyli-t* "ought not," *skal-a* "must not." Where *þú* "you" is attached as a suffixed *tu* to such a negative suffix, I have also separated it with such a hyphen (e.g., *skal-at-tu* "you must not" in st. 125 and 129).

I have written contracted forms of the words *ek* "I," *eru* "are," and *es* "is; who, which" with an apostrophe; for example, *þat's* "that which," *þrír'ru* "three are," *þyrfta'k* "I needed." I have not contracted these words in stanzas where they do not occur in contracted form in the manuscript (some early editors do). In some stanzas, both a contracted *ek* and the negative suffix are attached to one word, e.g., *fann'k-a* "I did not find" (st. 39). *Ek* can be contracted multiple times with one verb, as in *stǫðvi'g-a'k* ("I don't stop," st. 150) or *bjargi'g-a'k* ("I don't save," st. 152), with the contracted *'k* reduced to *'g* between unstressed vowels.

On those occasions when divergent spellings in the manuscript reflect not just typical Old Norse orthographic variation but rather interesting dialectal or archaic forms, I have not altered them—thus I have left *hálb* "half" rather than *hálf,* stanza 52; *hverb* "changeable" rather than *hverf,* stanza 74; and in several stanzas forms of *baztr* "best" rather than *beztr,* as well as the contraction *'s* (from *es* "is, who, which," an archaic form of *er*). Readers who are accustomed only to "classical" textbook Old Norse might be particularly surprised to encounter *Hávamál's* characteristic Old Norwegian first-person singular active verb ending *-um* with contracted *–'k* from *ek* "I." Such a form occurs, for example, in stanza 108 (*lǫgðum'k* "I laid" vs. textbook *lagða ek* or *lagða'k*), and also in the frequently repeated *ráðum'k* ("I advise," vs. textbook *ræð ek* or *ræð'k*) in stanzas 112–37.

As noted also in the Introduction, I write the I-umlauted version of the long vowel *ó* as *ǿ,* corresponding in form with the short version of the same vowel (*ø*), while English- and German-speaking editors usually render the letter *ǿ* as *œ* (a ligature of *o+e,* easily confused with the *æ* ligature from *a+e*).

Some early editors replaced every occurrence of *um,* meaning "about, over," or often simply a filler word, with the more archaic *of.* But the manuscript has both, and I have left *um* where the manuscript reads *um,* and *of* where the manuscript reads *of.* Many of the same early editors replaced *er* "is; who, which" and *var* "was" with their more archaic forms, *es* and *vas* respectively, but I have not followed this practice, preferring to print these words in the forms they have in our manuscript (however, the manuscript does have several instances of the contraction *'s* from archaic *es,* and I have of course left these intact). For those who might compare my text with transcriptions of *Hávamál* available online, the lack of these artificial archaisms will be one of the biggest differences, as websites tend to feature texts copied from very old (public domain) publications of the *Poetic Edda* in Old Norse.

1. In the *Codex Regius* manuscript, the title *Hávamál* can still be faintly deciphered in faded red ink above stanza 1.

Stanza 1 is also preserved as a quotation in *Gylfaginning,* the first section of Snorri Sturluson's *Prose Edda.* The *Prose Edda* was probably written in the 1220s AD. The stanza is not attributed to *Hávamál* or to Óđin there, but is simply a stanza spoken by Gylfi as he looks around an unfamiliar hall.

2. *Sjá* in line 3 is not "see," but rather an archaic masculine nominative singular form of *þessi*—"this (one), this (man)."

"On the threshold." The Old Norse in line 5 reads *á brǫndum,* which some early translators took erroneously as "on swords"— *brǫndum* is the dative plural of *brandr,* which can mean "sword," but given the nonmartial context, the meaning here is the more basic one of "something to be burned," i.e., firewood. Most likely the reference, as Björn Magnússon Ólsen proposed, is to something like the early Norwegian custom of a newly arrived guest sitting outside on the firewood until he was invited in. Because there is no close equivalent in English-speaking custom, I translate "on the threshold" to convey the sense of a guest not quite ready to come fully inside.

6. "A good supply of wisdom" is *mannvit mikit,* literally "much man-wit" in line 9, a phrase that seems somewhat homely in tone in Old Norse poetry and probably chosen for metrical reasons, alliterating with *mikit* "much" here and also in stanzas 10 and 11, and with *met-naðr* "pride," in stanza 79. Early translator Olive Bray rendered *mannvit* in stanzas 6, 10, and 11 by "mother wit," apparently a term for "common sense" in Bray's English but not one that has any relation to the actual Old Norse text. Unfortunately, the wording in Bray's easily discovered public-domain translation has caused some readers to misperceive an attempt to leave out a "mother" in these stanzas who in fact is not there at all in the original.

7. Line 6 reads, "In this way (*svá*) each (*hverr*) wise [one] (*fróðr*) 'noses himself' (*nýsisk*) forward (*fyrir*)." I have adjusted my English translation to accommodate this sense more concretely; in my original English translation in *The Poetic Edda: Stories of the Norse Gods and Heroes* (Hackett, 2015), I printed "That's how the wise get wiser," reflecting a more abstract sense of going forward through life that the text does not necessarily intend.

10–11. On *mannvit* "wisdom," see above under my comments on stanza 6.

12. The manuscript reads *sona* (genitive or accusative plural) rather than *sonum* (dative plural). This is probably due to attraction to the case of *alda* (compare the note on st. 21, below, for a more glaring example of case attraction), as *sona* in this context does not produce a grammatical sentence.

13. "A memory-stealing heron" is more literally *óminnishegri* "heron of un-memory." In this volume I have rendered the precise "heron" rather than simply "bird" (as in my original published translation in *The Poetic Edda: Stories of the Norse Gods and Heroes,* Hackett, 2015), as the mental image conjured by a heron is different from that conjured by a commonplace songbird. I have also made a more thorough examination of the uncommon verb *þruma*, which occurs here and in stanzas 17 and 30, and concluded that in all instances its basic meaning is close to English "brood," i.e., "stand motionless and silent, as if fixated," and so in line 2 of my translation I now render "broods" in place of my original "flies." This is in fact a good match for the behavior of a fishing heron, and this probably also brings us closer to the mental image of the original poet, who perhaps saw a huge heron lurking over the "pond" of a drinking party, lunging into its "waters" to pluck the memory out of the drinkers. In tribute to this curious bird of *Hávamál*, its opposite, *minnishegri* "heron of memory" was memorably proposed in 2007 as the Icelandic translation of "USB/flash drive," but rejected.

Gunnloð is the name of the "giant" (*jǫtunn*) woman Óðin seduces into giving him a drink of the mead Óðrerir, a story told also in *Hávamál* stanzas 104–10, and in more detail in Snorri Sturluson's *Prose Edda*.

14. The name *Fjalarr* is known from three other places in the Eddas. In the *Poetic Edda,* it is the name of the rooster who crows at Ragnarok in Jotunheim according to *Voluspá* stanza 41 (another rooster, named Gullinkambi, will crow in Valhalla, and another, unnamed, will crow in Hel), and it is the name of a being Óðin mentions in *Hárbarðsljóð* stanza 26 who may well be identical to the *Prose Edda*'s gigantic magician Útgarða-Loki. In the *Prose Edda*, *Fjalarr* is the name of one of the dwarves who kills Kvasir and mixes his blood with honey in order to make the mead known as Óðrerir. Because of Óðin's connection to the Óðrerir myth (see for instance *Hávamál* st. 104–10 and 141), the latter is the most intriguing possibility, but there is no record in any version of that myth of a visit that Óðin makes to Fjalar, though Fjalar's name might originally have belonged to someone else in the Óðrerir narrative and only later become attached to one of the dwarves. It is also possible that "the wise Fjalar" is in fact the rooster and that the house or place (the noun is not specified in the Old Norse text) where Óðin got drunk was simply Jotunheim more broadly. And if this Fjalar is the same as the Útgarða-Loki encountered by Thór in the *Prose Edda*, it is possible that Óðin also visited his hall and drank heavily there in a lost myth just as his son did in the surviving myth. There could also be yet a fourth Fjalar whose identity and exploits are not preserved in the surviving myths, or this stanza may refer to no specific myth at all, with the name chosen for metrical reasons.

17. The first half of this stanza contains obscure vocabulary, and a thorough examination of the individual words has persuaded me to change the way I translate it in this volume. The fool is *afglapi* here, almost "the confused one"; from the same root, compare *glepja*, "to perplex, confound," and *afglapa*, "to cause disorder (in a legal setting)." He "stares" (*kópir;* compare Modern Norwegian *kope* with this same meaning) "when he comes to a feast" (*er til kynnis kømr*).

Þylsk is the third-person singular mediopassive present of the verb *þylja*, whose basic meaning is "to make formal speech," so "to recite, speak." But in the singular mediopassive, as here, it must mean speech that has only the speaker as a beneficiary, thus probably "talks to himself." On *þrumir* in line 3, see under my comments on stanza 13. The gist of the stanza may be that a fool will be quiet when he arrives at a feast (in a different, perhaps more awkward way than the watchful guest of st. 7), but that his true foolishness will be revealed when he talks too much after he starts drinking, as talking too much rather than too little is more often a sign of foolishness in *Hávamál* (compare the silent man of st. 15 or the warning in st. 19 with the fool who talks too much in st. 27).

21. In the last line of this stanza, the manuscript reads *síns um máls maga*, with *máls* "measure" in the genitive case, apparently attracted into it by the fact that it is surrounded by two other words in the genitive case (compare the way someone might say "I never met my father's father's father's," with the last "father's" a simple error caused by attraction to the genitive/possessive form of the two before it). Here *máls* is thus emended to *mál* (accusative) so that it can act as the object of the verb *kann* "knows": literally, "an unwise (*ósviðr*) man (*maðr*) never *(ævagi)* knows (*kann*) the measure (*mál*) of his (*síns*) maw (*maga*)."

22. In the last line, the manuscript reads *at hann er vamma vanr* "that he is flawless," but this plainly contradicts the sense of the stanza. Like most editors, I have inserted a negative suffix on the verb *er* here.

27. The word *maðr* "man/person" does not appear in the first line in the manuscript. Because the line is incomplete without another word such as this, it was probably omitted by the scribe by accident, as the beginning lines of many stanzas in this section are very similar in wording.

30. I have adjusted my translation of this stanza to layer less of my own interpretation onto it, and in line with my conclusions on the word *þruma* (see under my comments on st. 13, above).

The lines of this stanza do not fit clearly together as it has been preserved. Lines 1–2 seem to be leading up to an admonition against mockery (perhaps like st. 31 or 132), but why would we not mock someone "even if" (*þótt*) he is a visitor? Perhaps the most lucid interpretation is to posit this as a caution against mocking those who are unfamiliar with the customs of a stranger's house.

31. I follow Guðmundur Finnbogason in emending *flótta* "flee" to **flátta* "mock." The latter word is not attested in the Old Norse period, but may be reconstructed based on *flåtta* "mock" in dialects of Modern Norwegian. If this was indeed an obscure word in the vocabulary of the *Codex Regius* manuscript's Icelandic scribe, the substitution of *ó* for *á* is unsurprising given the phonetic similarity of these vowels in mid-1200s Old Norse (when both were very likely long rounded back vowels).

32. Line 3 does not alliterate as it is preserved, but it does alliterate if the last word is emended to *vrekask*. In fact, this is strong evidence that the stanza is much older than the manuscript, as *vrekask* "fight each other" would have been the form of *rekask* before the regular sound change of *vr- > r-* had occurred in Old West Norse, which had occurred already before ca. AD 1000 based on alliteration patterns in datable skaldic poetry. Compare English *wreck* from the same root, with *wr-* cognate with archaic Old West Norse *vr-* (also still seen in East Scandinavian today, in Swedish *vrak* "wreck," Danish *vrag* "wreck," from the same root).

In line 2, *erusk* is a rare example of the reciprocal suffix *-sk* used on a form of the verb *vera,* "to be," thus "are to each other." The reciprocal suffix is also seen in line 3 in *rekask* "fight each other."

A literal interpretation of line 6 reads simply, "A guest (*gestr*) fights (*órir*) against (*við*) a guest (*gest*)." I rendered this with a more universal interpretation in my earlier published translation of this line ("where there's more than one, there's a fight"), but render it with plainer words closer to the original here, which also better maintains the "scene" of the original stanza, at a feast where two guests have gone from friends to enemies.

35. In the manuscript, the *skal* "shall/should" of the first line is not present, but the line requires some word of this type to be complete, and most editors have inserted *skal* as it fits the wording of similar stanzas in *Hávamál.*

36. Lines 1 and 2 do not alliterate with one another as would be expected, but the lines' meaning is so clear that no proposed emendation has ever won acceptance. Andreas Heusler suggested that these two lines are a time-worn saying that this pair of stanzas in *Hávamál* was constructed to complement; this might well be the case, or perhaps a later reciter or scribe was mistakenly influenced by such a well-known phrase when transmitting the stanza. Whatever has really happened here, Jónas Kristjánsson and Vésteinn Ólason point out that the *Codex Regius* scribe did not make a simple copying error in this stanza, as these two lines are repeated deliberately in the abbreviation *Bú er b.þ.l.s.* at the opening of stanza 37.

The "faulty roof" of line 5 is specifically *taugreptan* "roofed with rope, cord," rather than with something sturdier.

37. As reflected in my translation, a "bloody" (*blóðugt*) heart in Old Norse is in fact a wounded heart, and not, as contemporary English idiom might suggest, a lenient, liberal heart.

39. Where my fifth line reads *svá gjǫflan* "so giving," the manuscript reads simply *svági*, which gives no apparent sense in this sentence and is not a full line. Editors have long assumed that the scribe wrote *svá* "so" and then the first two letters of an adjective related to *gjǫf* "gift," but perhaps became distracted from the work and failed to finish writing the word after returning to it. *Gjǫflan*, the strong masculine accusative singular of *gjǫfull* "generous," fits the line well and thus is the choice of most editors.

41. In line 3, *sýnst* is the superlative of the adjective *sýnn*, "visible," thus a very literal reading of the line is "that (*þat*) is (*er*) most visible (*sýnst*) on (*á*) selves (*sjálfum*)."

47. In the manuscript, in addition to the typical use of the Younger Futhark rune for the letter *M*, named *maðr*, to stand for the word *maðr* "man/person" in its nominative form, the genitive form of the same word in line 6, *manns*, is rendered by the same rune with a letter *z* written over it (standing for *mannz*, a frequent spelling variant).

48. The second half of this stanza contains some obscure vocabulary. *Sýtir* is the third-person singular present form of *sýta* "wail, mourn," while *gløggr* is "miserly, ungenerous." A very literal reading of the last line gives "[an] ungenerous [man] (*gløggr*) mourns (*sýtir*) always (*æ*) about (*við*) gifts (*gjǫfum*)," i.e., he doesn't want gifts because they mean he will have to give something back. Reciprocity of gift-giving is an important norm in Old Norse culture evident in many myths and sagas. While my original translation of the last half of this stanza in *The Poetic Edda: Stories of the Norse Gods and Heroes* (Hackett, 2015) recast these lines as direct advice of a vaguer sort ("It's unwise / to spend your life worrying, / dreading your responsibilities"), in this volume I have rendered them more literally, retaining the third-person narrative of the original and conveying a more precise sense of this unwise man's dread of the specific responsibility that he has in medieval Norse culture to repay a gift.

49. "Scarecrows." The Old Norse reads *trémǫnnum*, "tree-men, wooden men," which could be religious idols rather than farmers' aids. But the plain sense of the stanza is that something that is only approximately a man is rendered truly a man by the addition of clothes, so I use "scarecrows" as one of the few examples of such a mannequin in present-day English-speaking culture. The sentiment is similar to a very literal interpretation of the saying "Clothes make the man."

In the manuscript, between the words *nøkkviðr* "naked" and *halr* "man" is written the Younger Futhark rune ψ for the letter *M*, standing for *maðr* "man/person." It is uncertain why the scribe wrote two words for "man" in a row; it was probably a simple lapse of attention, as the meter (and normal syntax) will abide only one. Here I print simply *halr*, as have most previous editors.

50. In line 3, the manuscript reads *hlýrar*, which is not a recognizable form of any Old Norse word. Virtually all editors emend to *hlýr-at* "doesn't protect."

"A person is the same way / if nobody loves him" or "if he loves nobody"? The Old Norse reads *Svá er maðr, / sá er manngi ann*, literally "so (*svá*) is (*er*) that (*sá*) man/person (*maðr*) who (*er*) nobody (*manngi*) loves (*ann*)." The case of *manngi* "nobody" is potentially ambiguous, as in this form it could either be the subject (nominative) or the object (dative) of the verb *ann* "loves." Meanwhile, *sá* "that (man)" is nominative, but because it must agree with *maðr* "man/person," this is not determinative. However, *manngi* is a common nominative form of this pronoun (see st. 71, 84, and 130, et al.), but seldom used in the dative (where *mannigi* is expected), so in my translation I favor the reading "if nobody loves him."

Note that *hvat* in Eddic poetry may mean not only "what," but also other question words, especially "how" and "why."

51. *Friðr* is "love, affection" rather than "peace" in the archaic language of *Hávamál*.

52. In the English translation I have the speaker win "friends," but in the original he wins *félaga*, accusative plural (or singular) of *félagi*, a word borrowed into English as "fellow" and often used admiringly in Viking-Age memorial runestones of a companion in arms.

53. The first half of this stanza is particularly strange in its grammar, and has probably been copied incorrectly at some stage in the transmission of this poem. *Lítilla sanda, / lítilla sæva* are words in the genitive plural—"of little sands, of little seas"—but it is not clear how these genitives/possessives are intended to relate to line 3, which literally reads "men's minds are little." My attempt to see the "seas" in line 2 as metaphors for the minds in line 3, with the "sands" of line 1 as perhaps a metaphor for the effects or deeds of little minds, is only one possible solution, but presumes that the text originally was intended to read something like **Litlir ('ru) sandar / litlir ('ru) sævar*, "Sands (are) little / seas (are) little," and even this does not produce an entirely clear point.

The meaning of line 6 is also unclear, particularly because *ǫld* is ambiguous; it can mean "era" or "a (kind of) people," and long vs. short vowels are not consistently distinguished in the manuscript, so we may be dealing with either *hvár* "each of a pair" or *hvar* "where, somewhere, everywhere." Attempting a literal translation with *hvár* produces "half (*hálb/hálf*) is (*er*) era? kind of people? (*ǫld*) each of a pair (*hvár*)." Are we to read "Each of the two eras is half"? or "Each of the two kinds of people is half?" What "half" refers to is not clear. Nor is it clear that either interpretation means something or fits with the first half of the stanza.

Attempting a literal translation with *hvar* produces "half (*hálb/hálf*) is (*er*) era? kind of people? (*ǫld*) somewhere/everywhere (*hvar*)." Can we read "Half of the era is somewhere" or "everywhere"? or "Half of the two kinds of people is somewhere" or "everywhere"?

My own tenuous reading of this tenuous stanza is developed from the latter interpretation, "Half of the two kinds of people is everywhere"; I take "the two kinds of people" to be the wise and the unwise, and I take *hvar* as "everywhere," suggesting that half of the people everywhere are wise and unwise, thus the average is moderately wise. However, this is hardly a definitive answer to the puzzle, and the confusing text suggests that the intended form and meaning of this stanza is lost.

In line 6, the spelling *hálb* for *hálf* "half" is very unique and probably reflects a divergent (Old Norwegian?) dialectal form. The Proto-Germanic root is **halβ-*, where in phonetic notation the Greek letter beta represents a voiced bilabial fricative much like that represented by the *v* in Spanish *cuervo*. Generally this Proto-Germanic consonant developed into a voiced labiodental fricative in Old Norse (phonetically [v], but spelled with an *f*), but in certain lesser-known dialects it might well have developed into a voiced bilabial stop [b] or remained a distinct phoneme, at least in certain positions. By way of comparison, German shows different outcomes of this consonant in different forms of one word derived from the same root; e.g., *die Hälfte* "the half" but *halb* "half" (adjective), *Halbzeit* "half-time."

54. A literal reading of the final line in the Old Norse order is, "who (*er*) well (*vel*) much (*mart*) know (*vitu*)." If this ought to be interpreted as "who know many things well," this line contradicts the sense of this stanza and the next two, and on that basis Björn Magnússon Ólsen (and subsequent scholars) suggested emending the final line to *er vel mart vitu-t* with the negative suffix on the verb, thus "who don't know much well." However, Ernst A. Kock compared *vel mart* to Swedish expressions of the type *väl varm* "just warm enough," and in my judgment this squares well with the gist of these three stanzas about the man who is *meðalsnotr* "middle-wise, a little wise"; such men are those "who (*er*) know (*vitu*) just enough (*vel mart*)." They are certainly not *unwise* men of the kind *Hávamál* constantly disparages. To reflect this reading more clearly, I have altered my translation of the final line from my original "are the moderately wise" to "are those who know just enough."

55. For a similar sentiment, see Ecclesiastes 1:18, "For in much wisdom is much grief: and he that increaseth knowledge increaseth sorrow."

57. In the manuscript, in addition to the typical use of the Younger Futhark rune for the letter *M*, named *maðr*, to stand for the word *maðr* "man/person" in its nominative form, the dative form of the same word, *manni*, is rendered by the same rune with a letter *i* written over it.

The word *kuðr* "wise, knowing" in line 5 is related to the verb *kunna* "know" (with the usual change of **nnr* > *ðr* in Old Norse, compare *maðr* "man/person" to its accusative *mann*). The cognate adjective in English is "couth," remembered now only in the negative "uncouth."

58. In line 2, *sá* does not appear in the manuscript but is supplied here by analogy with the similar wording at the beginning of stanza 59. The scribe wrote *ri* at the end of one line, then *sa* at the beginning of the next, spelling *rísa* "rise," and this seems to have caused the haplography (leaving off the apparent "doubling" of one word that would have appeared by writing a second *sa* again right after the first).

61. In my original translation in *The Poetic Edda: Stories of the Norse Gods and Heroes* (Hackett, 2015), I translated with an extra line in order to get the full effect of line 1, *þveginn ok mettr* ("combed and fed"): "with your hair combed / and a meal in your belly." Here I render the sense of this line in one line in English, "well-kempt and well-fed."

In line 5, I emend the manuscript's *in* (which is a form of the definite article, "the," but not one that gives any sense here) to *enn* "still, yet."

62–63. These two stanzas are written in reverse order in the manuscript, but above the first word of each (*snapir* and *fregna*, respectively), the scribe drew a symbol indicating that their order had been incorrectly switched. I follow most modern editors in printing them in the corrected order indicated by the scribe, rather than in the order as they are written in the manuscript.

64. The exact sense of the last half of this stanza, especially line 6 (*at engi er einna hvatastr*, "that no one is bravest of all"), is not certain; I have adjusted my English translation to render the Old Norse more literally and allow the reader to ponder it. It may be intended as a caution against bragging about or showing off one's abilities to the point that others are encouraged to compete with and defeat you. The same three lines (with *fleirum* "more; others" in place of *fróknum* "bold") occur also as the second half of stanza 17 of *Fáfnismál* (in the *Poetic Edda*).

66. The last line reads literally, "A hated one (*leiðr*) seldom (*sjaldan*) gets to (*hittir í*) a joint (*lið*)." The "joint" in question is a joint in meat.

In my earlier published translation (in *The Poetic Edda: Stories of the Norse Gods and Heroes,* Hackett, 2015), I proceeded from a very literal interpretation of this line, "A hated man seldom gets meat," and interpreted the "meat" as the food of hospitality that he is denied, thus I rendered "A hated man gets little hospitality." More plausibly, the last line is built around an idiom that is not meant to be taken this literally. The idiom in question, *hitta í lið* "get to a joint," is somewhat obscure but occurs elsewhere in Old Norse literature, seemingly with a meaning along the lines of "find the right moment."

67. The sense of this stanza is not immediately clear in the Old Norse, especially the last half, which might be rendered literally as "or (*eða*) if there hung (*hengi*) two (*tvau*) thighs (*lær*) at my trusted friend's house (*at ins tryggva vinar*) where (*þar's*) I (*ek*) had (*hafða*) eaten (*etit*) one (*eitt*)." Like in stanza 66 above, the "thighs" in question are pieces of meat to be eaten. In his edition, David A. H. Evans says Bo Almqvist suggested to him that this was sarcastic in tone; the host would feed the guest only if the guest could make the host's cellars fuller rather than emptier after the meal. Gísli Sigurðsson follows a similar interpretation in his edition of the *Poetic Edda*. I have followed the sense of this suggestion in my translation.

The strange-looking word *málungi* is *málum*, the dative plural of *mál* "mealtime," + the negative suffix *-gi*. The final *m* of *málum* is assimilated to *n* by the following *g*.

70. In line 2, *en sé ólifðum* "than (it) be (for the) dead" is an emendation for *ok sællifðum* "and (for the) happily lived" in the manuscript. This emendation was suggested in 1818 by Rasmus Rask and has been accepted by most editors since, as it lets line 2 alliterate with line 1 as expected, and forms a more meaningful contrast to make the point in line 3. Jónas Kristjánsson and Vésteinn Ólason emend to *ok sé illlifðum* "and (it) be (for the) badly lived" instead, which also gives good sense, favorably contrasting even a miserable life with death.

The literal meaning of line 3 is "[a] living [one] (*kvikr*) always (*ey*) gets (*getr*) [the] cow (*kú*)," i.e., between a living person and a dead one, only the living one will get something desirable. I have endeavored to render this sense of the line plainly in English.

The word *dauðr* in the last line has been interpreted in various ways; it could be the adjective "dead" (in which case, someone dead, probably the "rich man" of line 5, might lie outside the door) or it could be the noun "death" (in which case, death itself might wait outside the door for someone in the house). I have usually preferred the former explanation, but unlike in my translation in *The Poetic Edda: Stories of the Norse Gods and Heroes* (Hackett, 2015), I no longer favor the interpretation of the fire as a house fire, but rather a fire burning "for" (*fyr*) the rich man, i.e., for his benefit, but this rich man is dead outside the doors of his house, no longer able to enjoy it. This is a more economical translation of the somewhat difficult Old Norse of the last three lines, and accords better with the sense of the first three lines.

71. In line 2, the manuscript reads *hundarvanr*, potentially "dogless" (though **hundar* is not an expected form of *hundr* "dog"). Most editors emend to *handarvanr* "handless," which uses a known form of the word *hǫnd* "hand" and parallels the bodily impairments in the other lines.

In line 6, the Old Norse does not read as a question but as a simple statement: "No man (*manngi*) has use for (*nýtr*) a corpse (*nás*)." I translate it as a rhetorical question, as this strikes me as the natural way of phrasing such a blunt point in English.

72. *Bautarsteinar* or *bautasteinar* were memorial gravestones in pre-Christian Norway. Line 6 of the Old Norse is literally "unless (*nema*) [a] descendant/son (*niðr*) [may] raise [it] (*reisi*) in memory of (*at*) an ancestor/father (*nið*)." The word *niðr* (accusative *nið*) usually means "a son," but can mean another relation, especially in a direct line of ancestry or descent; clearly "father" is the relevant meaning of the second occurrence of the word here. The preposition in this line (with its accusative object *nið*) is probably a continuation of earlier *aft,* which is seen in many Viking-Age runestones with the meaning "in memory of," rather than the etymologically distinct but much more frequently seen preposition *at* "at" (which takes a dative object). Compare the beginning of the famous Rök runestone (early 800s AD): *aft uamuþ* (accusative) *stąnta runaR þaR* "these runes stand in memory of Vémóð."

73. The literal sense of the last couplet is "There is to me (= "I have," *er mér*) expectation (*væni*) of a hand (*handar*) into (*í*) each (*hvern*) coat (*heðin*)." "Each coat" is accusative rather than dative, which if not a scribal error might be meant to suggest movement into the folds of a coat or cloak. The stanza (which stands out for being in the *málaháttr* meter while the greater part of *Gestaþáttr* is in *ljóðaháttr*), and the thought, may be incomplete; the implication appears to be as I have rendered it, that the hand hidden by a cloak is suspect.

74. The first three lines appear to evoke a portrait of someone at ease on a short sailing trip. To read them very literally, "The one (*sá*) who (*er*) has confidence in (*trúir*) his meal/food provisions (*nesti*) is (*er*) happy (*feginn*) at night (*nótt*). The ship's (*skips*) yardarms (*rár*) are short (*'ru skammar*)." Because short yardarms would be used in a ship intended for short voyages, I translate the implication ("just a short distance to sail home"), allowing the emotional force of the scene to be clearer.

In line 3, I have the seaman "sail" home because of the reference to yardarms ("row" home in my earlier published translation).

In line 4, the spelling *hverb* probably reflects a dialectal form of expected *hverf* "changeable." See my comments on the form *hálb* under the notes for stanza 53.

75. *Margr verðr af ǫðrum api.* In the manuscript, this line reads *Margr verðr af lauðrum* (or *lǫðrum*) *api*, where the word *lauðrum/lǫðrum* is inexplicable and does not alliterate. I accept Sophus Bugge's emendation to *af ǫðrum*, meaning "from, because of others," which I interpret as "from, because of other fools." Some scholars, including David A. H. Evans, have instead amended to *af aurum,* i.e., "from, because of money," which also gives good sense.

In line 6, the rare verb *vítka* means "blame," while *vár* is the genitive singular of the feminine noun *vá* "woe, misfortune." Since one blames someone else for something in the genitive, a very literal reading of this line would produce "[one] ought not (*skyli-t*) blame (*vítka*) that [other man] (*þann*) for misfortune (*vár*)."

76–77. The opening two lines of these two stanzas, *Deyr fé / deyja frændr,* are also found in the last stanza of *Hákonarmál.* Because the author of that poem is remembered to history as Eyvind *Skáldaspillir* ("Plagiarist"), it is reasonable to assume that he is the borrower rather than the originator, suggesting that these stanzas may date to earlier than AD 961—although the possibility cannot be strictly ruled out that both *Hávamál* and *Hákonarmál* have incorporated these lines from an earlier source.

The livestock word *fé* generally denotes sheep in Modern Icelandic, but beef cattle in Old Norse (hence my rendering with "cows"). *Fé* is identical in form in both nominative singular and plural; the singular verb *deyr* "dies" in line 1 shows that here it is grammatically singular. However, the word has an inherently collective meaning, even when grammatically singular, much like English "cattle" or "stock."

Jónas Kristjánsson and Vésteinn Ólason cautiously suggest that stanza 76 might originally have been meant to follow directly after stanza 72.

For a similar sentiment and image to these stanzas, see Ecclesiastes 3:19, "For that which befalleth the sons of men befalleth beasts; even one thing befalleth them: as the one dieth, so dieth the other; yea, they have all one breath; so that a man hath no preeminence above a beast: for all is vanity." Likewise line 108 from *The Wanderer*, an Old English poem: *Hēr bið feoh lǣne, hēr bið frēond lǣne* "A cow is here temporarily, a kinsman is here temporarily."

78. "A rich man's sons." The Old Norse in line 2 literally reads *Fit-jungs sonum* "Fitjung's sons." Various explanations have been proposed for who Fitjung is; some have seen the name as a formation from the same root as *feitr* "fat," thus "Fatso" or something similar as an abusive term for a heavy man. Magnus Olsen suggested that it might be related to the name of a particularly important and wealthy farm in Viking-Age Norway. But whatever the specific way that the name came to be, it is clearly intended as a shorthand for someone wealthy, whose sons were betrayed by the "faithless friend" that is money.

80. Óðin is identified in the Old Norse text of this stanza as *Fimbulþulr*. *Fimbul* means "mighty, terrible," often with a sense of the supernatural; the *fimbulvetr* is the "mighty winter" that will accompany Ragnarok, the death of the gods, and in stanza 140 Óðin declares he knows nine *fimbulljóð* "mighty songs," i.e., magical spells (but in st. 103, *fimbulfambi* is simply "a (terrible) fool"). For remarks on the meaning of *þulr*, see my comments on stanza 111, below.

The runes are called *rúnum / . . . inum reginkunnum* "the runes of divine origin." In the Noleby runestone (ca. 500s AD), we read *runo . . . raginakundo,* "rune of divine origin," and in the Sparlösa runestone (ca. 800s AD), *runąR þaR rakinukutu* "those runes of divine origin," in both instances a representation in runic orthography for the precisely cognate phrase in an earlier stage of the language. In the translation of this stanza in *The Poetic Edda: Stories of the Norse Gods and Heroes* (Hackett, 2015), I translated "they are gifts of the Æsir," but have found "they are of divine origin" a more satisfactorily exact translation of this adjective. Note that this separate clause is not part of the Old Norse original, where *reginkunnum* "of divine origin" is simply an attributive adjective describing *rúnum* "runes," but I find no acceptable way to render "of divine origin" as an attributive adjective in English.

81. In the translation of this stanza in *The Poetic Edda: Stories of the Norse Gods and Heroes* (Hackett, 2015), I translated "don't praise your wife until she's buried" in order to create a rhyme with "married" two lines later. However, the Old Norse plainly reads *brennd* "burned," i.e., cremated, and while the central meaning of the line and the whole stanza is something similar to "don't count your chickens until they hatch" (and thus the specific way the wife's funeral is conducted is not significant to its sense), the reference to cremation is in fact an important indication of the age of this stanza, because cremation was not practiced in medieval Christian Scandinavia.

83. I accept David A. H. Evans' explanation of the dog being fed *á búi* ("at dwelling," but *someone else's* dwelling, to judge by occurrences of this phrase elsewhere in Old Norse literature) as effectively an instruction to let it fend for itself.

84. The second half of this stanza is also preserved as a quotation in chapter 21 of the *Saga of the Foster-Brothers* (*Fóstbrǿðra saga*). It is not attributed to the poem *Hávamál* or to the god Óðin in the saga; there it is simply "a little saying people repeated about cheating women, that came into his [Lodin's] mind then." Editor Jónas Kristjánsson dates the composition of this saga to ca. AD 1260, which regrettably is too close to the writing of the *Codex Regius* manuscript to be of any help in determining the date of the poem itself.

88–89. I have reversed the order of these two stanzas (but indicated the original order in their numbering), as stanza 89 appears to continue the list of things not to trust from stanza 87.

90. *Friðr* is "love, affection" rather than "peace" in the archaic language of *Hávamál;* in this volume I have modified my original published translation ("Take care not to love / a deceitful woman") to reflect faithfully the descriptive rather than admonitory tone of this stanza. *Óðum* is the strong masculine dative singular form of the adjective *óðr* "wild, mad, crazy, angry," which shares the same root as Óðin's own name.

This stanza is clearly of Norwegian origin; reindeer are not native to Iceland, and descendant forms of the word *þáfjall* "mountain in thaw" are known from Norwegian dialects but not from Modern Icelandic.

92. *Frjá* is an archaic verb meaning "love, be in love" (it is related to *friðr*, "love," later "peace," and ultimately to Old Norse *frændi* "kinsman," English *friend*). A very literal reading of line 6 gives "that [man] (*sá*) gets (*fær*) who (*er*) loves (*frjár*)"; here I render it with an interpretation based more closely on this reading and more complementary to and less redundant with lines 4–5 than my original published translation ("you will win her if you praise her").

93. For the second half of the stanza, a literal reading of the Old Norse original would be "Lust-beautiful (*lostfagrir*) looks (*litir*) often (*opt*) intoxicate (*fá á*) [a] wise [man] (*horskan*) which (*er*) do not (*né*) intoxicate (*fá á*) [a] foolish [man] (*heimskan*)."

94. In the manuscript, line 4 reads *horskan* "wise" (accusative singular) rather than *horskum* (dative plural), but the latter is expected because of the case governed by the preposition *ór* "out of" and the context.

In line 6, *mátki* is the masculine nominative singular weak form of *máttugr* "mighty." Note also the double specification of the noun here: *sá inn mátki munr,* literally "that [one] the mighty love."

95. Here I have printed the "classical," textbook Old Norse forms *engi* and *engu* "none, nothing" where the manuscript has *aung* and *aungu*, respectively, probably representing phonetically *øng* and *øngu*. This pronoun does occur in a bewildering variety of forms, but these are fairly rare.

97. *Billings mey.* I have translated this as "Billing's daughter," because *mær/mey* means "a girl, a young woman" and generally implies a daughter when used as a term of relationship in this way. However, it is also used in the sense of "romantic partner" or even "wife" at times, so these relationships are possible as well. Nothing of Billing or his unnamed "girl" is known outside of these stanzas, though *Billingr* is included in the list of dwarves' names in the late version of *Voluspá* in the manuscript called *Hauksbók*. It does not seem likely that this is the same Billing, as in early Old Norse literature dwarves seem to be always male (the *dœtr Dvalins* "daughters of Dvalin" alluded to in *Fáfnismál* are perhaps an exception), and are never love objects for the gods. Billing and his daughter in *Hávamál* are probably either humans or "giants" (*jǫtnar*), who are often desired by the gods.

Old Norse frequently uses the language of bright light to describe beautiful women, and the adjective *hvítr* "white" is part of this vocabulary. *Hvítr* "white" is not used to label any normal human skin tone in Old Norse, but instead implies a cowardly paleness in mortal men, while in women and gods (such as Heimdall and Baldr) it suggests radiant beauty (almost the same figure of speech in English). I thus translate *sólhvíta* "sun-white" as "fair as a sun-ray," maintaining the salient identification of the woman as beautiful rather than either literally luminescent or simply "white."

In line 6, I have altered my original translation from *The Poetic Edda: Stories of the Norse Gods and Heroes* (Hackett, 2015) ("unless I could live with that woman") to reflect the rawer literal meaning: "unless I could live next to that body."

98. In line 3, the form *vilt* meaning "(you) want" is late, but exactly as written in the manuscript; this late form also appears in stanza 130. The expected *vill* appears in stanza 44 and (with negative suffix) in stanza 114.

In line 5, the manuscript reads *einir* "alone" (masculine nominative plural) not *ein* (neuter nominative plural), but the latter is expected because a woman is talking about a man and a woman rather than two men, who "alone" ought to know about the affair. Here, I also follow Finnur Jónsson in emending the manuscript's *viti* (third-person plural, subjunctive) to *vitim* (first-person plural, subjunctive), making "we" the subject—"unless (*nema*) we alone know (*ein vitim*)," and I have adjusted my English translation to reflect this emendation more clearly.

100. Given the context, *vílstígr* is almost certainly to be read with the first element as *víl* "misery, problem," thus the embarrassed Óðin is shown his "miserable way," not his *vilstígr* "desired way" (with *vil* "will, desire," with a short *i*). However, because the latter is printed in the influential Neckel-Kuhn edition, many other editors and translators follow it.

101. Many modern commentators (including the most thorough, David A. H. Evans and John McKinnell) and translators take the dog (*grey*) of line 4 as a female dog left on the bed to mock Óðin's lust for the woman. However, this is much too elaborate given the simple way Óðin is repulsed the other two times (by the woman's lie in stanza 98, and by the fighters in stanza 100), and it relies heavily on the identification of the dog as female, which is not guaranteed by the grammatically neuter term *grey*. While *grey*, which is related to the first part of the English word *greyhound*, is often used as a term of abuse for men and women alike (invoking cowardice, in a sense more akin to "cur" than to "bitch" in English), its occurrence here as the choice of term for "dog" likely has more to do with its alliteration with *góðu* in line 5.

Óðin as the storyteller is convincingly obsessed with complimenting the woman he says he lusted for; she is *in horska mær* "that wise girl/woman" in stanza 96, *innar góðu konu* "that good woman" in stanza 101, and she is *góð mær* "[a] good girl/woman," *it ráðspaka / . . . fljóð* "that wise woman," and *it horska man* "that wise girl/lady" in stanza 102, and in each of these instances the adjective he uses is in alliteration with another word or words. That *grey* "dog, cur" is the alliterating word chosen in stanza 101 is hardly surprising, given the contempt with which he would regard the watchdog left in his would-be lover's chambers to alert her other guardians to his intrusion.

102. A very literal translation of the memorably rhythmic lines 5–6 produces "when (*er*) I (*ek*) led (*teygða*) the (*it*) wise (*ráðspaka*) woman (*fljóð*) into (*á*) bad deeds (*flærðir*)." Because Óðin's story makes it evident that he did not succeed in leading her into bad (sexual) deeds, I render "tried to seduce."

In line 9, the manuscript reads *vætkis* (not *vætki* "nothing," which is an emendation made by many editors since the nineteenth century); this could conceivably be interpreted as an adjectival use of this pronoun ("no, none"), inflected in the genitive to agree with genitive *vífs*, giving something like "and (*ok*) I (*ek*) had (*hafða*) thus (*þess*) no (*vætkis*) woman (*vífs*)." However, it would be difficult to find parallels for such a use of *vætki(s)*, or for *hafa* "have" with a genitive object (though *fá* "get" takes a genitive object when used of "getting," i.e., "marrying," a woman), and it is probably best to emend *vætkis* to *vætki* and read the line as "and (*ok*) I (*ek*) had (*hafða*) nothing (*vætki*) of that (*þess*) woman (*vífs*)." In the English translation, my rendering of *víf(s)* as "wife" is based not on the cognate (the Old Norse word indicates a woman but not necessarily a married woman) but rather on the context of Óðin's disappointment.

106. *Létumk* in line 2 is probably to be read as the relatively uncommon suffixation of *mér* or *mik* "me" as *-(u)mk* to a verb that it is not the object of; "I let (*lét*) Rati's (*Rata*) mouth (*munn*) make (*fá*) room (*rúms*) for me (*mér,* "hidden" in the suffix *-(u)mk*) and (*ok*) gnaw (*gnaga*) rock (*grjót*)," with *um* as a metrical filler word. Note that in line 5, *mér* "me," the object of the prepositions *yfir* "over" and *undir* "under," is also suffixed as *-(u)mk* in *stóðumk;* a literal reading of lines 4–5 gives "giants' (*jǫtna*) roads (*vegir*) stood (*stóðu*) over (*yfir*) and (*ok*) under (*undir*) me" (*mér,* "hidden" in the suffix *-(u)mk*).

Rati is the name of the drill that Óðin uses to access the cave Gunnloð lives in, according to the fuller version of the Óðrerir story preserved in Snorri Sturluson's *Prose Edda*. This stanza of *Hávamál* implies that he escapes, rather than gains entry, by this means, but disagreements of this sort between variants of one myth are exceedingly common. In the English translation, I have rendered *Rata munn,* literally "Rati's mouth," by "Rati's tusk," emphasizing the part of an animal mouth that is comparable to a drill.

In contrasting stanza 106 with stanza 32, we see strong evidence that *Hávamál* cannot originally have been the work of one poet. In stanza 32 (as noted above), the alliteration in line 3 is only valid if the Old West Norse change of *vr > r* had not occurred when it was composed. But in stanza 106, the alliteration is only valid after this consistent sound change, which had happened by ca. AD 1000. Before this change, *Rata* in line 1 must have been **Vrata* (compare Old Danish *vraade,* "to burrow, dig," from the same root) and would not have alliterated with *rúms* in line 2.

107. A literal translation of lines 1–2 would read, "I (*ek*) have (*hefi*) used/enjoyed (*notit*) well-purchased (*vel keypts*) beauty/appearance (*litar*) well (*vel*)." I interpret "the well-purchased appearance" as a disguise Óðin somehow acquired in order to seduce Gunnloð successfully. Other commentators have seen Gunnloð herself as the "well-purchased beauty," but it is not usual for abstractions or qualities to be used to name people in Old Norse (unlike in English where one might say, e.g., "She's a beauty" or "She's a vision").

The last line of this stanza in the manuscript reads, *á alda vés jarðar* "on men's sacred place's earth's," which provides no object for the preposition *á*. Like most editors, I have therefore emended *jarðar* to *jaðar* "rim" (accusative singular), and interpreted "men's sacred place's rim" as the rim of Miðgarð, the realm inhabited by human beings in the Norse cosmos. This does not actually accord with the detailed Óðrerir story as told by Snorri in the *Prose Edda*, but the version in *Hávamál* is divergent from that story in other ways too. In my original translation in *The Poetic Edda: Stories of the Norse Gods and Heroes* (Hackett, 2015), I rendered the last two lines as "is rescued / from the clutches of the giants," which avoided the problem of where the mead was delivered by emphasizing where it had been rescued from (the central point of the story).

The name *Óðrerir* is probably from the root of *óðr* "wild, mad, crazy, angry" (the same as the root in Óðin's own name) + *hrǿrir* "stirrer, mover," thus roughly "what stirs (the mind, the person) to wildness, madness." Alternately, the first element could be based on the noun *óðr*, "poetry." It is not unusual for a long vowel to be shortened and even to change its quality in a secondarily stressed syllable, and the vowel represented here as *ǿ* is represented by numerous different spellings; for both these reasons the name is spelled in various ways in Old Norse. For its part, the *Codex Regius* manuscript spells it *Óðreri(r)* in stanzas 107 and 140 of *Hávamál,* and I have done likewise.

109. Two names are used for Óđin in this stanza, *Bǫlverkr* and *Hávi*, although one can be read simply as an accusatory description in this context. First the *hrímþursar* "frost-giants" come to the hall of *Hávi* to ask for advice from *Hávi*; this means "the high one" and it is of course the name of Óđin that occurs in the title *Hávamál* (see the Introduction for more on this title and an alternative explanation of the name).

The frost-giants then inquire about the "evildoer." In the fuller version of the Óđrerir story preserved in Snorri Sturluson's Prose Edda, "evildoer" (Old Norse *Bǫlverkr*) is the name Óđin assumes with Suttung and Gunnlođ. It is also one of the names Óđin claims as his own in the poem *Grímnismál* in the *Poetic Edda*.

In the earlier version of my translation, printed in *The Poetic Edda: Stories of the Norse Gods and Heroes* (Hackett, 2015), I had the frost-giants ask "news" of Óđin rather than his advice. The word *ráđ* can indeed mean other types of speech, but here I am using its most typical meaning of "advice" (the advice is, presumably, on the subject of locating the "evildoer" or *Bǫlverkr*). I have also capitalized *Evildoer* and placed it in quotes in the English translation, to reflect its double function as accusation and as name.

110. The specific type of oath Óđin swore is a *baugeiđr*, "ring-oath." In the beginning of *in heiđnu lǫg* "the heathen laws" preserved in the *Hauksbók* manuscript version of the Old Icelandic *Landnámabók* "Book of Settlements," it is stipulated that men must swear legal oaths (calling on the gods Frey, Njorđ, and "the almighty one of the Æsir") on a ring belonging to the *gođi* or priest-chieftain. Oaths sworn on rings are also frequent in other myths and sagas.

"But who can trust Óðin?" Very literally, "How (*hvat*) shall one (*skal*) trust (*trúa*) his (*hans*) promises (*tryggðum*)?"

111. "On the wise man's chair." No more specific translation than "wise man" for Old Norse *þulr* seems possible; the word is archaic already in the language of the 1200s when the Eddas and sagas are written down, and it is never used in those works to describe contemporary individuals. It is related to Old English *þyle*, which likewise seems already archaic in a poem such as *Bēowulf*, where it is used as the title of Ūnferð, the sharp-tongued advisor and spokesman for King Hrōðgār. In Old Norse, the word has associations with old age in many of the contexts in which it appears. *Þulr* is related to the verb *þylja*, which appears in line 1 and means "to recite, speak," and also appears in stanza 17 in a less dignified context in the third-person singular mediopassive present *þylsk* "talks to himself."

Urð is the foremost of the three Norns, female beings who determine the fate of all life. Her well is at the base of the great tree Yggdrasil, according to *Voluspá* in the *Poetic Edda*.

As in stanza 109, "Óðin's hall" is once again literally "the hall of the high one (*Hávi*)."

112. Starting with this stanza, most of the other stanzas are assumed to begin with the same opening formula of four lines beginning *Ráðum'k þér, Loddfáfnir* . . . as they are written with abbreviations that indicate a repetition of the formula. In my translation of the formula, I have rendered "if you take my advice" in line 2 rather than "that you take my advice," because though *at* is strictly translated as "that," the verb in the line is subjunctive and thus indicates some uncertainty that the audience will in fact do it.

116. In the manuscript we read the opening formula abbreviated as *Ráðum'k þ. l. f. ē.*, followed by line 5: *Á fjalli eða firði . . .* The abbreviation *ē* would typically be read as *en* "but," which has led some editors to print this stanza (and sometimes more stanzas in *Loddfáfnismál*, or even all of them) with the formula beginning *Ráðum'k þér, Loddfáfnir, / en þú ráð nemir . . .* "I advise you, Loddfáfnir / but you take my advice . . ." rather than *Ráðum'k þér, Loddfáfnir, / at þú ráð nemir . . .* "I advise you, Loddfáfnir / that you take my advice. . . ." However, whatever the motivation for writing *ē* in the abbreviated formula here, this version of the opening does not make as much sense, and I have printed all the stanzas of *Loddfáfnismál* with the same opening formula as in stanza 112, the only stanza where it is written out in full.

119. *Vegs* "road's" rather than *vex* "grows" is what occurs in the manuscript; the emendation to *vex* is accepted by virtually all editors.

120. *Gamanrúnum* is the dative plural of *gamanrúnar*, meaning either "joyful runes" or simply "joyful talk." Compounds with *-rúnar* (dative plural *-rúnum*) pose a notorious problem for translators because of this double meaning. In my translation in *The Poetic Edda: Stories of the Norse Gods and Heroes* (Hackett, 2015), I took the meaning as "runes" because of the occurrence of *líknargaldr* "healing spell" in the same stanza, but in fact this is fairly difficult to sustain with the verb *teygðu* "draw in, attract to," which makes more sense with the meaning "talk." Given that *gamanrúnum* also occurs in stanza 130, and even in as magical a context as *Sigrdrífumál*, stanza 5 (see the *Poetic Edda*), and in both instances it plainly means "joyful talk," I have adjusted my translation to "joyful talk" in this stanza as well.

124. Lines 4–5 are difficult; a probable literal reading would be "Everything (*allt*) is (*er*) better (*betra*) than (*en*) [it may] be (*sé*) to be (*at vera*) [with] deceptive (*brigðum*)," with the word *brigðum*, a dative form of the adjective *brigðr* "deceptive," probably having the sense "(with) deceptive (people, friends)," thus "Anything is better than being with deceptive people/friends." In this volume, I have tried to render these lines with a sense somewhat closer to the original (emphasizing that the company of liars, not the lie itself necessarily, is the source of discomfort) than I was able to in *The Poetic Edda: Stories of the Norse Gods and Heroes* (Hackett, 2015).

Line 6 is pithier in Old Norse but impossible to render both concisely and precisely in English; the very literal translation would be "That one (*sá*) is not (*er-a*) a friend (*vinr*) to others (*ǫðrum*) who (*er*) speaks (*segir*) only (*eitt*) wanted (*vilt*)," i.e., "what is wanted," i.e., "what you want to hear." Here I take *vilt* in line 6 as neuter accusative singular of *vildr* "wanted."

127. There is an ambiguous abbreviation in the manuscript in line 6, where some read *kveðu þat bǫlvi at* ("call it evil"), and others *kveðu* *þér bǫlvi at* (roughly, "call [it] evil for you"). I favor the former reading, as the latter seems strangely altruistic in *Hávamál.*

In the original version of my translation in *The Poetic Edda: Stories of the Norse Gods and Heroes* (Hackett, 2015), I rendered *bǫl* "evil" as the particular evil of "war" owing to the presence of "enemies," but now favor an interpretation of it as a more general "evil" because the advice is clearly more widely applicable. I have also adjusted my translation of the verb *kannt* (from *kunna*) to its more basic sense of "know, recognize."

129. The more literal reading of lines 7–8 is "men's sons, i.e., men (*gumna synir*), become (*verða*) like (*glíkir*) a *gjalt* (*gjalti,* dative singular)." The Old Norse word *gjalt* is borrowed from Old Irish *geilt.* William Sayers has described the curse of the Old Irish *geilt* as that of an inexperienced warrior, struck mad by terror when he hears war cries, who then flees his first battle and thereafter lives for years in the woods like a wild bird, frightened of humans, hunting with nails grown to claws, and sometimes growing feathers. The Old Norse use of the motif of the *geilt/gjalt* (and this borrowed word) is not so intricate in the Icelandic sagas, where the man who becomes a *gjalt* is often simply paralyzed by fear temporarily (hence my earlier translation of this stanza in *The Poetic Edda: Stories of the Norse Gods and Heroes,* where I rendered "may get turned to stone" in line 8). However, as the bulk of *Hávamál* was probably composed much earlier than the prose sagas, in a time when contacts with Old Irish culture were more intimate, it is plausible that the more complex and lasting madness of the Irish *geilt* is meant to be evoked here.

130. For the late form *vilt* meaning "(you) want" see under my comments on stanza 98.

134. "Never laugh / at an old man." The alliterating Old Norse lines are more specific: "Never laugh at a gray-haired *þulr*." For more remarks on the meaning of *þulr*, see my comments on stanza 111, above.

The last three lines of this stanza are among the most difficult in *Hávamál*. The three verbs are all related to the notion of hanging: *hangir* "hangs," *skollir* "swings," *váfir* "waves." *Hám* and *skrám* are dative plurals from *há* "dried skin" and *skrá* "dried skin," respectively. *Vílmǫgum* is more difficult to parse; it may be the dative plural of a compound *vilmagi* "(animals') guts-stomach," as suggested by Jónas Kristjánsson and Vésteinn Ólason, or the dative plural of the attested word *vílmǫgr* "miserable son," apparently a term of abuse.

In my translation in *The Poetic Edda: Stories of the Norse Gods and Heroes* (Hackett, 2015), I rendered these lines "From those who hang with dried skins / those who swing with dried skins / those who wave with dried skins." In this translation, I have adjusted these lines to reflect the singular verbs and the interpretation of *vílmǫgum* as a term for people rather than another synonym for skins. What the lines mean is a different matter; who hangs with dried skins or with despicable people is not clear, nor is there any obvious connection to the five lines above, which have an unambiguous message of listening to the counsel of the old. One possible interpretation is Rolf Pipping's: that the man (in his capacity as *þulr*?) is hanging (as Óðin himself does in st. 138) near men who are already dead (the "dried skins") and other men who have not yet died (the "despicable men," who are perhaps criminals sentenced to be hanged).

135. The manuscript reads *geyja* "to spite," but I follow David A. H. Evans' emendation of this infinitive to the imperative *gey* + the negative suffix *-a,* therefore meaning "Don't spite."

136. The first half of this stanza has caused trouble for many scholars. My own first interpretation took the *tré* "tree" in line 1 as a hanging tree that one *skal ríða* "shall ride, shall hang from" but this is a fairly tenuous use of the vocabulary present. *Upploki* in line 3 is particularly difficult, but is probably a noun formed to the verb phrase *lúka upp,* thus "an (act of) opening." David A. H. Evans suggests taking the *tré* as the beam on a door, thus producing a sense like "That (*þat*) beam (*tré*) is (*er*) strong (*rammt*) which (*er*) shall (*skal*) swing (*ríða*) at (*at*) opening (*upploki*) for everyone (*ǫllum*)." The verb *ríða* "ride" can indeed mean "swing (open)," so this is an economic use of the vocabulary present, but the point is not immediately clear. Perhaps the idea is to join the idea of hospitality (let the door be open for all) with a note of caution (but the door must be strong, to close behind a bad guest). Joined with the less ambiguous second half, which encourages us to be generous lest we be cursed, this might well be the right gist.

137. This stanza is evidently a list of traditional remedies against different harms, though the specific remedies here are hard to parallel in other Old Norse texts. In line 11, I accept David A. H. Evans' suggestion that the manuscript's *haull* might stand for **hǫll,* an otherwise unattested Old Norse cognate of Norwegian *hyll*, meaning "elder-tree." This has the particularly strong advantage of being in line with the natural remedies in the stanza's other lines. Otherwise it would be expected to stand for *hǫll*, "hall," in which case the meaning might be that a hall or home will avail against family quarrels, though it is hard to see much sense in this.

Line 12 lacks the parallel structure of the other lines, "remedy *við* affliction," and so I print it parenthetically in the Old Norse text and move it to the end in my English translation. I take the meaning to be "[one] shall (*skal*) call on (*kveðja*) the moon (*mána*) with regard to hatreds (*heiptum*)." In fact, it is difficult to say what *heiptum* "hatreds" is doing here; it might be that one is supposed to call on the moon as a remedy against hate in the same way the other remedies are called on against other afflictions. But because this line is not structured the same way as the remedy lines, and because *kveðja* "to call on" has a legalistic sense, I take the meaning as effectively "summoning" the moon as a witness, hence my English translation.

138. Óðin hangs for nine nights, and nine recurs again and again as the most significant number in Norse mythology: Heimdall has nine mothers, there are nine "worlds" or realms, Óðin does the work of nine slaves in Snorri's version of the Óðrerir story, etc.

Óðin is strongly associated with the spear; he is *geirs dróttinn* "lord of the spear" in a poem from the mid-900s AD attributed to Egil Skalla-Grímsson, and already in the early 800s Bragi Boddason knew the name of Óðin's own magical spear (made for him by dwarves, according to Snorri's *Prose Edda*) as *Gungnir*. While this stanza does not specify that Óðin was wounded with Gungnir, the natural intuition is that the lord of the spear "gave" himself to himself with his own weapon.

King Víkar is also said to be "given" to Óðin when Starkað sacrifices him in nearly the same way in the *Saga of Gautrek* (*Gautreks saga;* see elsewhere in this volume). The similarities of the two sacrifices are great, and it is reasonable to infer that Óðin in *Hávamál* is speaking of sacrificing himself to himself by a similar means to how men might be sacrificed to him, and with similar language. In yet another comparable scene, in *Styrbjarnar þáttr* "The Story of Styr-bjorn," King Eirekr *gafsk honum* "gave himself to him [Óðin]" in exchange for victory in a battle, but stipulated that he would not die for another ten years; Óðin later gives him a reed (which, like in *Gautrek,* will turn into a spear when used) to throw over his enemies, instructing him to say *Óðinn á yðr alla* "Óðin owns you all."

Some popular modern depictions have Óðin hanging upside-down, however there is no reason to suppose this is the case based on the language of this stanza. The verb used, *hekk,* is the regular first-person past singular form of *hanga,* "to hang," which when used of men elsewhere in Old Norse literature routinely means to hang right-side-up by the neck.

In the manuscript, the first word of the last line reads *hvers* "whose" rather than *hvar's* "where" but I have emended to the latter given that it makes better sense in context. A very literal translation of the last line would then be, "where *(hvar's)* it *(hann)* runs *(renn)* from *(af)* roots *(rótum)*." David A. H. Evans suggests that it might be emended to *hverjum* instead, in which case the translation would be "from *(af)* what *(hverjum)* roots *(rótum)* it *(hann)* runs *(renn)*."

The last two lines are very similar to a couplet about the world-tree in the poem *Fjǫlsvinnsmál*, which reads *en fáir vitu / af hver-jum rótum renn* "but few know / from what roots [the tree] runs," and though the tree is called *Mímameiðr* in that poem, the nat-ural assumption is that the tree Óðin hung upon was the world-tree, whose name *Yggdrasill* contains the common Óðin name *Yggr* ("Terrifier"). In fact, the name *Yggdrasill* has long been interpreted as "Óðin's horse" (because *drasill* is a poetic term for horse), and therefore to represent Norse gallows humor: Óðin "rode" the world tree (hanged men are often said to "ride" the tree or gallows they hang from in Norse literature). However, it is difficult to make grammatical sense of the name in that case, because the first part of the name would be expected in the genitive/possessive form *Yggs* if this were in fact "*Yggr's*/Óðin's horse." And because the tree is more often called *Yggdrasils askr* "ash-tree of *Yggdrasill*," there may be a more complicated, undiscovered myth behind the occurrence of Óðin's name *Yggr* here.

Anatoly Liberman has proposed that *Yggdrasill*, which he ren-ders "terrible god-horse," was in fact earlier a name for Óðin's horse Sleipnir, and that *askr Yggdrasils* "ash-tree of *Yggdrasill*" began as a kenning (an allusive, metaphorical poetic name); *askr* "ash-tree" is common in kennings for men, so "the man of *Yggdrasill*" would originally be Óðin. Liberman proposes that over time the mean-ing of this kenning was forgotten, which resulted in the (orig-inally mistaken) re-association of this *askr* with the world-tree, and thus the application of the name *Yggdrasill* to the tree rather than the horse. Of course, all such ideas are speculative, though

Liberman's proposal has the distinction of being the most plausible from the perspective of historical semantics and Old Norse poetic practice.

So the form of the tree's name, which is often adduced as evidence that it was Óðin's hanging-tree, is in fact not strong evidence in itself. Ultimately, the text of *Hávamál* tells us only that Óðin hung on a tree with enigmatic roots—that it was the world-tree is a compelling and likely inference, but not a given.

139. I have read *seldu* from the manuscript as *søldu* "(they) relieved (hunger or thirst)" rather than *seldu* "(they) gave, sold," as this reading makes the clearest sense with the preposition *við* "with" (while this may appear arbitrary, in fact occurrences of the vowels *ø* and *æ* are often represented by an *e* in the *Codex Regius*). A very literal translation might then be "they relieved (*søldu*) me (*mik*) with (*við*) bread (*hleifi*) nor (*né*) with (*við*) a drinking horn (*hornigi*)." Old Norse *né* "nor" is often placed between two things that are both denied, thus "They didn't relieve me with bread/food, nor did they relieve me with a drinking horn/drink."

Another plausible reading, favored by Anthony Faulkes, is *sældu* "(they) gladdened."

The word *rúnar* is conventionally translated "runes," and because of the following stanzas (142–44) that clearly reference runic letters, it is probable that this is the correct translation in this stanza as well. However, *rúnar* can also mean "secrets," and the possibility that this was the original meaning in this stanza cannot be completely excluded.

140. The name of Óðin's maternal grandfather is spelled *Bǫlþorn* rather than *Bǫlþórr* in the *Prose Edda*, which seems more likely as a giant's name ("curse-thorn" rather than "curse-Thór" or "curse-thunder"), and thus I printed it that way in *The Poetic Edda,* but in this volume I have followed the spelling in *Hávamál* in the *Codex Regius* manuscript. Who Bolthór's son (Óðin's maternal uncle) might have been is unknown.

The name Óðrerir is used both for the drink itself and for its container; here the container is evidently meant. This stanza also appears to point to the existence of a very different myth of how Óðin won Óðrerir than the one alluded to in stanzas 104–10 and described in Snorri Sturluson's *Prose Edda.*

141. The verb *frævask* in line 1 is difficult, as it is very rare in this mediopassive form, and the only straightforward interpretation is "to become (or make oneself) fruitful/fertile"; the root is shared by the noun *fræ* "seed." In the original version of my translation in *The Poetic Edda: Stories of the Norse Gods and Heroes* (Hackett, 2015) I translated line 1 as "My imagination expanded," reading an *intellectual* fruitfulness into this obscure statement, but here I translate it literally in order to allow the reader to ponder what it might mean, which is by no means clear.

142. In Old Norse, this stanza identifies Óðin as *Fimbulþulr* (as in st. 80; see my comments on that stanza above) and as *Hróptr* (possibly "famed god"), a name for Óðin that occurs in several other poems in the *Poetic Edda*, including *Voluspá*, *Grímnismál*, and *Lokasenna.*

143. The manuscript text of lines 2–3 reads, *en fyr álfum Dvalinn Dáinn ok dvergum fyrir,* but above *Dáinn* and *Dvalinn* the scribe drew a symbol indicating that their order had been incorrectly switched. This would still produce the unusual order *en fyr álfum Dáinn / Dvalinn ok dvergum fyrir,* with *ok* "and" between *Dvalinn* and *dvergum* "dwarves," but I follow most editors in moving *ok* before *Dvalinn* to preserve the symmetry with the rest of the lines in this stanza and the usual rhythms of Old Norse poetry.

Carolyne Larrington has suggested that the "I" at the end of this stanza is a human speaker, the one who carved runes for humans, parallel with the named beings who carved for the gods, the elves, the dwarves, and the giants in the preceding stanzas.

144. Given the context, situated among other stanzas about runes, and the fact that the first half of this stanza's content certainly seems connected to runes ("writing," "reading," and "painting" especially, but even "testing," given the comparison to st. 80), one could infer that the second half concerns runes as well.

However, it is less clear that the last half refers to actions to be done to runes than that the first half does, and I am not convinced that it does. *Biðja* means "ask" but also specifically "pray," and *blóta* is a verb of religious action that generally means "worship, sacrifice." Pointing in a darker direction, *sóa* "offer, sacrifice" can mean "kill" in some contexts, as it clearly does in the last line of stanza 109, and Anatoly Liberman has made a strong case that *senda* "to send" can also be read as "make a human sacrifice, kill" in some contexts in Old Norse—note that Óðin tells Starkað, *Nú skaltu* senda *mér*

Víkar konung "Now you must *send* King Víkar to me," in the selection from the *Saga of Gautrek* printed later in this volume. However, *senda* and *sóa* seem to have no such dark associations in stanza 145 immediately following, so it is unclear that they ought to be read with such sinister undertones here, and I am hesitant to do so.

145. In Old Norse, Óđin's name in this stanza is given as *Þundr*, a name Óđin claims as his own in Grímnismál in *The Poetic Edda* (st. 46). While it is nearly irresistible to see the English word "thunder" in this name, I have lately concluded that it is more likely to be an archaic past participle to the verb *þenja*, and thus to mean "stretched." Óđin has been "stretched" by his hanging (*Hávamál*, st. 138–39). The English word "thunder" is in fact an exact cognate not to Old Norse *Þundr* but to the name of the Norse god *Þórr* (Thór).

The time "when [Óđin] rose up / and returned again" is likely after he had fallen from the tree, as described in stanza 139 (if *Þundr* does indeed mean "stretched," then the use of that name in this stanza also calls to mind this related myth).

Metrically, this is one of the strangest stanzas in the poem; it begins with five lines of *ljóðaháttr* (without the expected sixth line) and ends with four lines of *fornyrðislag,* the Eddic meter typically used in third-person narrative poems such as *Voluspá.* Since there is no narrative link between the two sections, a good case has been made by John McKinnell that the last four lines were drawn from another lost poem about Óđin's sacrifice that told the tale from a third-person perspective. This is very plausible, but why these lines were inserted in this particular place in *Hávamál* is not easy to discern.

For a similar sentiment to this stanza, compare Ecclesiastes 5:5, "Better is it that thou shouldest not vow, than that thou shouldest vow and not pay."

146. *Mannskis mǫgr.* Here the genitive/possessive singular of *maðr* "man/person," *manns* "man's," has the negative suffix *-ki* attached to it together with a repeated possessive ending *-s*, resulting in "no man's" (as also in, e.g., st. 114). *Mǫgr* is "son," thus *mannskis mǫgr* "no man's son" allows the poet to say "no man" with a full alliterating line.

148. Berserkers, who are associated with Óðin by Snorri Sturluson in his *Saga of the Ynglings* (*Ynglinga saga*) as "Óðin's men," often use a spell like this one in the sagas. For example, in the *Saga of Gunnlaug Worm-tongue* (*Gunnlaugs saga ormstungu*), the hero has to conceal a second sword during the beginning of his fight with a berserker so that he will still be armed after the berserker magically disables the one he sees him carrying (chapter 7).

151. I follow Hugo Pipping in reading *rótum rás viðar* as "roots of a gnarled tree," seeing *rás* as related to the dialectal Swedish word *vrå* "cross-grained, gnarled." I have also adjusted the English translation to reflect this interpretation more specifically. Several previous editors have emended to *rótum rams viðar* "roots of a strong tree," though a strong tree seems a vaguer image than a gnarled one.

The carving of runes on a tree root in order to cause harm, and the use of magic to repel that harm onto the one who intended it, both have parallels in the sagas. The hero of *Grettir's Saga* (*Grettis saga*) is killed by the infection he sustains after cutting his foot when he tries to chop a tree root that an old woman had carved runes on, reddened with her blood, spoken spells over, and then sent into the ocean with the words *Verði Gretti allt mein at,* "Be of all harm to Grettir" (chapter 79). But in *Walking-Hrólf's Saga* (*Gǫngu-Hrólfs saga*), the dwarven wizard Mondul uses some kind of carving magic (runes are not explicitly named) that causes twelve sorcerers who are casting a spell on his allies compelling suicide to kill themselves instead (chapter 28).

152. The fire that burns "bright" in my line 4 is not a direct translation, despite the similar sound, of the fire that burns *breitt* ("broadly") in the Old Norse text, but rather an equivalent description of the intensity of the fire, as I am unaware of fires described as "broad" in English. "It cannot burn so huge" might be more literal, but seems awkward in English as well.

Together with the spells in stanzas 154 and 157, the effect of this spell is among those that Snorri Sturluson mentions when he enumerates Óðin's magical powers in the *Saga of the Ynglings* (*Ynglinga saga*).

154. Together with the spells in stanzas 152 and 157, the effect of this spell is among those that Snorri Sturluson mentions when he enumerates Óðin's magical powers in the *Saga of the Ynglings* (*Ynglinga saga*).

155. Like most editors, I emend the manuscript's *þeir villir* ("they wild/lost," masculine nominative plural) to *þær villar* (feminine nominative plural) to agree with the feminine *túnriður* "farm-riders, witches" that these words evidently refer back to (there is no apparent masculine word for them to refer to).

The last half of the stanza poses a curious problem of interpretation. Lines 4–5 may be read straightforwardly in a literal translation as "I (*ek*) work/cause (*vinn'k*, with *ek* repeated as *'k*) so (*svá*) that (*at*) they (*þær*) go (*fara*) wild/astray/lost (*villar*)." But the last two lines contain only genitive plurals, "of their home-skins" (*sinna heimhama*, from *hamr*, "skin") and "of their home-minds" (*sinna heimhuga*, from *hugr* "mind"). It would appear that Óðin's spell causes these flying sorceresses to get lost, but what is the underlying belief or myth behind their inability to find their "home-skins" and "home-minds"?

Perhaps the witch's mind or spirit separates from her body to move around freely, a notion similar to some later folkloric beliefs described by Bente Gullveig Alver about a separable consciousness (called *hug* in Modern Norwegian, from Old Norse *hugr*) that leaves the body and can wander in a different "skin" (*ham* in Modern Norwegian, Old Norse *hamr*), often that of an animal. A witch can sometimes consciously direct her own *hug* in folklore, which may be what the *túnriður* are doing in this stanza of *Hávamál*. In that case, this spell that makes the witch get lost relative to her "home-"*hamr* and her "home-"*hugr* may be understood as a magical measure that prevents her body and mind from re-uniting when she has sent her mind away from her body in the guise of an animal.

157. Together with the spells in stanzas 152 and 154, the effect of this spell is among those that Snorri Sturluson mentions when he enumerates Óðin's magical powers in the *Saga of the Ynglings* (*Ynglinga saga*).

Óðin has a strong and ancient association with hanging and hanged men; see stanza 138 and my commentary on it, in addition to the scene from the *Saga of Gautrek* (*Gautreks saga*) translated in this volume. Among Óðin's many names in pre-Christian Norse poetry, he is called *gálga valdr* "lord of the noose," in a poem by the skáld Helgi the Trusty (mid-900s AD), *gálga farmr* "load of the noose" by Eyvind the Plagiarist (also mid-900s), and Thorbjorn Brúnason (ca. AD 1000) calls him *hanga heimpingaðr* "the one who visits the hanged man at home." Snorri Sturluson adds *hangaguð* "god of the hanged man," and the name *Þundr* may be an allusion to his association with hanging as well (see under my comments on st. 145).

While the individuals in question may not be victims of hanging, Óðin certainly awakes and speaks with the dead on occasion, as he does with dead witches in the poems *Voluspá* and *Baldrs draumar* (see *The Poetic Edda: Stories of the Norse Gods and Heroes*, Hackett, 2015).

158. Other poems and many sagas record that in a ritual similar to baptism, newborns were sprinkled with water when they were given names. The poem *Rígsthula* (see *The Poetic Edda: Stories of the Norse Gods and Heroes*, Hackett, 2015) reports that new parents "sprinkled [the newborn] with water" (*jósu vatni*, st. 7, 19, and 32), and likewise in the *Saga of the Volsungs* (*Vǫlsunga saga*) a young hero "was sprinkled with water and given the name Sigurð" (*var . . . vatni ausinn með Sigurðar nafni*, chapter 13). However, the verb used elsewhere is *ausa* "sprinkle, splash" (third-person past plural *jósu*), while this stanza of *Hávamál* uses *verpa* "throw," which might mean that the naming ritual for newborns is not what is meant in this stanza—and though *verpa* might be chosen purely to alliterate with *vatni, ausa* and its forms may also alliterate, as words that begin with vowels or *j* are sometimes allowed to alliterate with words that begin with *v.*

Line 2 of the Old Norse text (translated in line 3 of the English translation) reads *þegn ungan. Ungan* is "young," while *þegn* is a word loosely translated as "man" but loaded with associations in the Viking Age, and used especially of settled landowners (as extensively discussed by Judith Jesch in *Ships and Men in the Late Viking Age*). However, the word may be chosen for purely metrical reasons here, as *þegn* alliterates with *þréttánda* in the preceding line.

Thus, because the vocabulary of the stanza differs from the usual way of discussing the naming ritual for newborns—but also may only differ in this way because of metrical needs—I am no longer as confident as I once was that the naming ritual is what is pictured here. Thus I render lines 2–3 literally as "if I throw (*verpa*) water / upon a young man (*þegn*)," rather than "if I sprinkle water / upon a new-born boy," as I did in the original translation of *Hávamál* that appeared in *The Poetic Edda: Stories of the Norse Gods and Heroes* (Hackett, 2015).

160. "They knew Óðin" or "Thought/knowledge for Óðin"? The word *hyggju* could be the accusative singular of the feminine noun *hyggja* meaning "thought, thinking, knowledge," or it could be a defective form of the verb *hyggja* "to think, know." In the original translation of *Hávamál* in my *The Poetic Edda: Stories of the Norse Gods and Heroes* (Hackett, 2015), I favored the latter, but now favor the former on account of the symmetry with lines 4–6 and the fact that the verb *hyggja* is rarely used with a direct object.

In this stanza, Óðin is called *Hróptatýr*; *Hróptr* itself occurs as his name elsewhere (including in *Hávamál* st. 142), and *týr* "god" is a frequent element in his names.

If there was ever any other information about the dwarf Thjóðreyrir, it is lost. His name may be an error here; Jónas Kristjánsson and Vésteinn Ólason point out that lines 1–2 lack alliteration (a name beginning with *f-* would be expected in line 2, to alliterate with *fimmtánda* in line 1).

Curiously, Óðin uses the same words as in line 3, *fyr Dellings durum* "before Delling's doors," in five of the riddles he poses to King Heiðrek in the *Saga of Hervor and Heiðrek* (*Hervarar saga ok Heiðreks*, forthcoming in my translation from Hackett).

161. In line 5, I translate *hvítarmri*, literally "white-armed," as "lovely armed." See under my comments on stanza 97 discussing the use of *hvítr* "white" to mean "beautiful" when applied to women and gods.

162. The return of Loddfáfnir here has befuddled generations of scholars. Some, including John McKinnell, have suspected that at least some of the lines in this stanza were inserted by the compiler of *Hávamál* in order to create continuity between the different constituent poems, but there is no apparent justification for Loddfáfnir to resurface in this stanza in particular.

Elizabeth Jackson has argued that in fact all the stanzas from 111 on are addressed to Loddfáfnir, citing certain verbal echoes between stanzas (see under the comments on st. 164, below, for an example), parallels with the structure of the advice-poem *Sigrdrífumál* later in the

Poetic Edda, and seeing the discussion of runes in stanzas 139–44 as a fulfillment of the promise in stanza 111 that "I heard about runes."

164. For my revised translation in this volume, in line 2, I have followed my decision in stanzas 109 and 111 and rendered *Háva hǫllu* as "Óðin's hall" rather than the specific name *Valhalla* (Old Norse *Valhǫll*), which does not appear in *Hávamál.*

Line 4 reads *óþorf ýta sonum* "for the harm of men's sons (=humans)" as originally written in the manuscript, but this is a direct contradiction of the prior line. Already in the margin of the manuscript itself someone (generations later) wrote *jǫtna* as a replacement for *ýta*, producing "for the harm of giants' sons (=giants)." Most editors, with the notable exception of Judy Quinn, accept this emendation.

In line 7, I have altered my original published translation "joy to you who learn them" to reflect in English the strong verbal echo of the *Loddfáfnismál* opening formula (*njóta mundu ef þú nemr,* "you'll profit if you learn it") and of stanza 162, line 8 (*nýt ef þú nemr,* "they'd profit you if you learned them"). The verb in question, *njóta,* is "to derive good (from), profit (from), enjoy."

The majority of scholars hold that this final "summing-up" stanza is the work of the editor who assembled the constituent parts of *Hávamál.* Jónas Kristjánsson and Vésteinn Ólason disagree, arguing that if so, the editor would also have composed an opening stanza for the whole poem as well. Elizabeth Jackson, meanwhile, argues that all of stanzas 111–64 are one unified composition, in which case stanza 111 provides an opening stanza with a similar tone to the grand closing stanza here.

Related Texts

Darraðarljóð

The poem *Darraðarljóð* is included in the text of chapter 157 of *Brennu-Njáls Saga* "Saga of Burned Njál," the longest and one of the most famous of the Sagas of Icelanders, during a vision of a character named Dorruð. *Darraðarljóð* would thus mean "Dorruð's Poem/Song," but the poem is probably much older than the saga in which it is framed, and rather than a man's name the meaning of the poem's title was likely originally intended as "Song of the Spear (*dǫrruðr*)."

Below, I include the immediately preceding text of the saga as well.

*

> On Friday morning it so happened on Caithness that a man named Dorruð walked outside. He saw twelve people riding together to a wealthy woman's quarters, and then they all disappeared. He looked through a window that was there, and he saw that there were women inside and they had set up a loom. They were using men's heads for the weights, men's guts for the weft and yarn, and swords and arrows for the rods. They spoke these stanzas:

1. The threads are open,
   meaning death in battle!
   It's raining blood
   from the crossbeam.
   Now a gray weave

of men is here,
which the son-killer's
lady-friends
will fill in
with red cloth.

2.   The weave is woven
with men's guts,
and weighed down hard
with their heads.
Blood-covered spears
are the rods,
the beam is iron-covered,
and arrows shake it.
We make our war-weave
out of swords.

3.   Hild is weaving
and Hjorthrimul,
Sanngríd, and Svipul
use drawn swords.
Spear will break,
shield will break,
a helmet-chopping sword
will ruin shields.

4.   We spin, we spin,
a weave of spears,
which the young king
had before.

We'll go forward
and wade into the fight,
where our friends
exchange weapon-blows.

5.   We spin, we spin
a weave of spears,
and then we follow
the young king.
Guð and Gondul,
who guarded him,
saw the fighters'
bloody shields.

6.   We spin, we spin
a weave of spears,
where able fighters'
flags are flying.
Let us not
be careless with *his* life;
we Valkyries have
the *choice* of the dead.

7.   Those armies
from the settlements
in the far peninsulas
will rule these lands;
I say the rich king
is marked to fall.

Now the ruler falls,
pierced by spearpoints.

8. And now the Irish
    will suffer miserably,
    that agony will never
    leave the Irish people.
    Now the weave is woven,
    the field is bloody,
    this enormous loss of life
    will become famous.

9. Now it is horrible
    to look upon
    as bloody clouds
    cross the sky.
    The very sky is red
    with men's blood,
    while we battle-watchers
    sing away.

10. We spoke right
    about the young king,
    many victory-songs,
    we sing well!
    Let the one listening
    learn our spear-flight song,
    let him say it
    to others!

11.   Let us leave, ride our
      bare-back horses hard,
      with drawn swords
      we'll ride away.

Eiríksmál and Hákonarmál

Eiríksmál ("Words of/for Eirik") is a poem in Eddic style commissioned in memory of Norwegian King Eirík Bloodaxe (Old Norse *Eiríkr blóðøx*) by his wife Gunnhild after his death in AD 954. The poem is not preserved in its entirety, but the nine stanzas that survive paint a picture of Óðin preparing Valhalla for Eirík's arrival while speaking to Bragi (a god of poetry) and the famous human heroes Sigmund and Sinfjotli (well known from *The Saga of the Volsungs*).

Hákonarmál ("Words of/for Hakon") is a poem of similar style and content, composed in honor of Norwegian King Hákon the Good (Old Norse *Hákon góði*) after his death in AD 961 at the Battle of Fitjar on the island of Stord. The poem, which is attributed to Eyvind the Plagiarist (Old Norse *Eyvindr skáldaspillir*), is preserved in its entirety in Snorri Sturluson's *Saga of Hákon the Good* in the saga collection *Heimskringla*. This poem also presents a vision of Hákon's welcome arrival at Valhalla, and concludes with a stanza that has very similar language to the famous stanzas 76–77 of *Hávamál*. Despite the theme of the poem, Hakon the Good was a Christian.

EIRÍKSMÁL

1. Óðin said, "What is this
    thunderous noise?
    I awoke before dawn,
    and Valhalla was quiet.
    I woke up my champions,
    I told them to rise,
    to spread hay on the benches
    and prepare the beer,
    I told the Valkyries to serve wine
    for a king's arrival.

2. "It looks like kings of men
    are arriving from Miðgarð,
    some excellent warriors!
    My heart is cheered to see them.

3. "Bragi! Do you hear it,
    as if a thousand men
    or more were coming?"
    Bragi said, "The benches creak
    with the crowds sitting on them,
    as if Baldr were coming home."

4. Óðin said, "I don't want to hear
    foolishness from you, wise Bragi.
    You know well who it is—
    this noise means it's Eirík!

That king is coming here,
to me in Valhalla.

5.   "Sigmund! Sinfjotli!
     Get up quickly,
     and greet the king!
     Tell him to come in,
     if it's Eirík—
     I have great hope that it is."

6.   Sigmund said, "Why are you more eager
     to see Eirík than any other king?"
     Óðin said, "Because Eirík
     has reddened swords and carried
     a bloody blade across many lands."

7.   Sigmund said, "Why not give him
     victory, if he is so outstanding?"
     Óðin said, "Because I never know
     when the gray wolf Fenrir
     will come to the walls of Ásgarð."

8.   Sigmund said, "Hail, Eirik! You are welcome,
     and come freely to our hall.
     I'd like to ask what kings
     those are—who follows you there,
     coming in from the battle?"

9.   Eirik said, "Five kings,
       and I'll tell you the names of them all.
       And I myself am the sixth."

HÁKONARMÁL

1.   Óðin sent his Valkyries,
       Gondul and Skogul,
       to choose a king
       from the Yngling clan
       to go with Óðin,
       and live in Valhalla.

2.   They found Bjorn's brother,
       Hákon, in his armor,
       a great king beneath
       his war-banners;
       the spears stood ready
       and shook, the battle began.

3.   That killer of kings
       called on men from every
       part of Norway,
       and went forth to fight.
       That good king, enemy of Danes,
       stood beneath his helmet,
       with his good band
       of Norwegian warriors.

4. That leader of men
    stripped off his armor,
    threw his chain mail
    to the earth before the battle.
    In his golden helmet,
    the cheerful king
    would defend his realm
    from his enemies.

5. The good sword
    in that king's hand
    struck through armor
    as if through water.
    Wooden shields creaked
    and burst into fragments,
    and their swords thundered
    as they split the skulls of men.

6. Shields and heads
    were crushed
    under marching feet
    and the swords of Hákon's men.
    There was war
    on the island of Stord,
    the kings reddened shields
    in their enemies' blood.

7. Wounds spread
    like wildfire,
    and axes prescribed

the ends of lives.
A tide of wounds came in
on a beach of swords,
and a flood of spears
drowned the shore of Stord.

8. Clouds swirled in the sky
above the battle,
they fought hard
at the red edge of heaven.
Spears whined through
the sky above the fighters,
and many a man knelt
and died from swordplay.

9. The dead warriors sat,
pierced with arrows,
with broken shields
and their swords in hand.
That army did not walk
cheerfully on the roads
to Óđin in Valhalla.

10. The Valkyrie Gondul spoke,
leaning on a spear:
"Óđin's army grows,
now that Hákon
and his great army
are invited to Ásgarđ."

11. The king heard
    what the famous Valkyries
    were saying on horseback.
    They were clad in helmets
    and they were cheerful,
    holding shields at their side.

12. Hákon said, "Geirskogul,
    why did the battle go this way?
    The gods owed me a victory."
    The Valkyrie replied,
    "We did give you victory,
    and your enemies have fled."

13. The great Valkyrie Skogul said,
    "It's time for us to ride
    to the green homes of the gods
    and tell Óđin
    that the king is coming
    to pay him a visit."

14. Óđin said,
    "Hermóđ! Bragi!
    Go and greet the king.
    A ruler is coming,
    looking like a champion,
    here to my hall."

15. The king spoke then,
    newly arrived from battle,

standing soaked in blood:
"Óđin seems evil-minded
to me, for I seem to perceive
what his intentions are."

16. Bragi said, "You are welcome
among all Óđin's chosen.
Now accept the gods' good ale.
And look, killer of kings—
eight of your brothers
are already here."

17. Hákon said, "I would like
to keep my weapons.
But take good care
of my helmet and armor,
and keep them
within my reach."

18. Then it was proven
how well the king
had honored the holy places,
when all the gods
made Hákon welcome
to their halls in Ásgarđ.

19. It was a good day
when such a king was born,
with such a spirit!
The time of his rule

will always be remembered
as a good era in Norway.

20.   Fenrir, the monstrous wolf,
       will come unchained
       and terrorize Miđgarđ,
       before another king
       as good as Hákon
       rules in Norway.

21.   Cows die, family die,
       and our lands and properties
       are destroyed by enemies.
       Since Hákon left us
       to be with the heathen gods,
       the Norwegian people suffer.

An Excerpt from The Saga of Gautrek

The Saga of Gautrek (Old Norse *Gautreks saga*) includes a scene in chapter 7 in which Óđin not only dispenses his blessings on the hero Starkađ, but also encourages him to sacrifice King Víkar in a manner strikingly similar to his sacrifice of himself to himself in *Hávamál* 138–39. Below, I include my translation of this scene together with some explanatory glosses in brackets.

*

King Víkar sailed from Agder north to Hordaland with a large army. They stopped at a cluster of some small islands for a long time with a strong wind against them. They threw a *spánn* [literally a "chip of wood" or even a "spoon," apparently used in an unknown divination ritual] looking for a favorable wind, and the result they received was that Óđin wanted them to hang a man from their army. Then everyone in the army drew lots, and it was King Víkar who lost. Everyone went silent at that, and they decided that on the day after, their counselors would discuss this difficult predicament.

That night, around midnight, Horsehair-Whisker [*Hrosshárs-Grani*] woke up his foster-son Starkađ and told him to come with him. They took a small boat and rowed over to another small island. They went into the forest and found a clearing there in the trees, and in the clearing there were numerous people and an assembly had been gathered. There were eleven people seated in chairs, with a twelfth that was empty. The assembly was called to order, and Horsehair-Whisker took his seat, and the others greeted him as Óđin. He said that the judges would now determine the fate of Starkađ.

Then Thór spoke up and said, "Álfhild, Starkađ's mother, chose a crafty giant to be the father of her child instead of Thór of the Æsir, and so I decree that Starkađ will have neither a son nor a daughter, and thus will be the last of his family line."

Óđin said, "I decree that he will live three lifetimes."

Thór said, "I decree that he will commit a shameful crime in each one."

Óđin replied, "I decree that he will have the best weapons and clothes."

Thór said, "I decree that he will never own land."

Óđin said, "I decree that he will have plenty of money."

Thór said, "I decree that he will never think it's enough."

Óđin said, "I give him victory and outstanding skill in every battle."

Thór said, "I decree that he will receive a horrible injury in each one."

Óđin said, "I give him the art of poetry, so that he will compose poems as effortlessly as he speaks."

Thór said, "He will not remember what he composes."

Óđin said, "I decree that he will be the favorite of all the noblest of men and the best."

Thór said, "He will be hated by the middle class."

Then the judges declared that all this would come to pass for Starkađ as it had been decreed, and the assembly was declared at an end.

Then Óđin and Starkađ went back to their boat. Óđin said to Starkađ, "Now you will repay me well, foster-son, for the good I did you there."

"Yes," said Starkađ.

Then Óđin said, "Now you must send King Víkar to me, and I will tell you how." And Starkađ agreed to this, at which point Óđin put a spear in his hand and told him that it would look like a reed to other men.

Then they went back to the army, and the new day had just dawned. In the morning all the king's counselors had a meeting to discuss the situation. They came to a consensus, deciding that they would conduct some kind of mock sacrifice, and Starkađ told them of his plan. There was a fir tree near them, and a high tree trunk near the fir. There was a soft, bent branch hanging down from the fir tree.

Now the servants prepared food for the men, and in the process a calf was cut up and disemboweled. Starkađ ordered them to take some of the calf's intestine, and then he went up onto the tree trunk and draped the soft branch of the fir tree over the trunk and then knotted the intestine around the branch. Then he said to the king, "Now the hanging-tree is ready for you, lord, and I don't think it looks too dangerous. Now come here, and I'll put this 'noose' around your neck."

The king stepped forward up onto the tree trunk, and then Starkađ put the intestine around his neck and then stepped down off the tree trunk. Then he took the reed and stabbed it at the king and said, "Now I give you to Óđin." ['Nú gef ek þik Óðni.'] And Starkađ let go of the fir tree branch.

At that point, the reed turned into a spear, and it stabbed through the king's body, and the tree trunk he had been standing on fell away beneath him, and the calf's intestine turned into a strong rope, and the fir tree branch rose higher, lifting the king among the top branches of the tree, and he died there. That place has been called Víkarsholm since.

Glossary of Names

Note that the alphabetization of this glossary is based on American rather than Scandinavian conventions. *Æ* is treated as *A+E*, *Ð* is treated as *D*, *Ø* and (in Swedish and Modern Icelandic place-names) *Ö* are treated as *O*, *Ǫ* is printed as and treated as *O*, and *Þ* is printed as and alphabetized as TH. The length of vowels is printed but ignored in alphabetization. More details on the anglicization of Old Norse used in this volume's translations can be found in the Introduction.

Where the original spelling of a name in Old Norse is different from the more anglicized spelling used in the translated narrative, or when an English-language or present-day Scandinavian form of a place-name has been substituted for the Old Norse name, I have indicated the Old Norse spelling in parentheses following the name.

Æsir, the chief family of the Norse gods (including Óðin), sometimes contrasted vaguely with another family of (apparently subordinate) gods, the Vanir.

Agder (*Agðir*), district in southwest Norway.

Ásgard (*Ásgarðr*), the "gods' enclosure," the realm occupied by gods and contrasted chiefly with *Midgard* (the "middle enclosure," realm of human beings), *Jotunheim* (the realm of the *jǫtnar* or "giants"), and *Hel* (the realm of the dead).

Ásvid (*Ásviðr*), a "giant" (*jǫtunn*). The name is not known from any other source.

Baldr, a famously handsome god and son of Óðin, who was killed through the treacherous plotting of the scheming god Loki.

Bestla, Óðin's mother.

Billing (*Billingr*), an unknown male being (man? "giant"? dwarf?) whose "girl" (daughter or wife, probably the former) is unsuccessfully courted by Óðin in *Hávamál*, st. 96–102. This name is also given to a dwarf in the list of dwarves' names in the late version of *Voluspá* in the manuscript *Hauksbók*.

Billing's daughter, my translation of Old Norse *Billings mær* ("Billing's girl"), an unnamed woman (probably Billing's daughter) who is courted by Óðin in *Hávamál*, stanzas 96–102.

Bolthór (*Bǫlþórr*), maternal grandfather of Óðin. In *Hávamál* (st. 140), Óðin says that he learned magic from his "famous son," thus from an uncle of Óðin's, but this uncle's name and identity are unknown.

Bragi, a minor god associated with poetry, possibly to be identified with the human poet Bragi Boddason who flourished early in the 800s AD.

Dáin (*Dáinn*), seemingly an elf (Old Norse *álfr*), though this term is obscure in Old Norse. The name is given to a deer in the poem *Grímnismál* in the *Poetic Edda*.

Delling (*Dellingr*), a name that occurs in *Hávamál* (st. 160). It occurs in some lists of dwarf names, as well as in *Vafthrúdnismál* in the *Poetic Edda* as the name of the father of *Dagr* "Day." The words *fyr Dellings durum* "before Delling's doors" also occur in five of the riddles Óðin poses to King Heiðrek in *The Saga of Hervor and Heiðrek*.

Dvalin (*Dvalinn*), a dwarf. Though this is a fairly frequent dwarf name, it is also given to a deer in the poem *Grímnismál* in the *Poetic Edda*.

Eirík Bloodaxe (*Eiríkr blóðøx*), a king of Norway, d. AD 954.

Fenrir, the huge wolf that will break free of his chains and eat Óðin during Ragnarok, the final battle between the gods and their enemies.

Fjalar (*Fjalarr*), the host of a feast mentioned in *Hávamál* (st. 14). What relationship this Fjalar might have to the rooster of the same name mentioned in the poem *Voluspá* (see the *Poetic Edda*, p. 11), or to the dwarf of the same name who murders Kvasir in the *Prose Edda*, is unknown.

Geirskogul (*Geirskǫgul*), a Valkyrie's name.

Giant, traditional English translation of Old Norse *jǫtunn* (plural *jǫtnar*) or *þurs* (plural *þursar*), a term for the greater supernatural beings who are the gods' chief rivals. English "giant" implies that they are distinguished by their great size, but in fact *jǫtunn* in Old Norse has no implications of size, and there is no indication in the Eddas that the giants are larger than the gods or routinely look different from them. Many of the gods, including Óðin and Thór, have giant mothers, and giant women who marry gods become goddesses, so the giants are in no way a different "species" from the gods, and the lines between them are sometimes difficult to draw.

Gondul (*Gǫndul*), a Valkyrie's name.

Gud (*Guðr*), a Valkyrie's name (meaning simply "battle").

Gunnlod (*Gunnlǫð*), the "giant" (*jǫtunn*) woman who guards Óðrerir, the mead that makes its drinker a poet. She is seduced by Óðin in a story related briefly in *Hávamál* and more fully (in a different variant) in Snorri Sturluson's *Prose Edda*.

Hákon the Good (*Hákon inn góði*), a king of Norway, d. AD 961.

Hermód (*Hermóðr*), a resident of Valhalla. In Snorri Sturluson's *Prose Edda*, he is a son of Óðin who rides to Hel to bargain for Baldr's release after his death.

Hild (*Hildr*), a Valkyrie's name.

Hjorthrimul (*Hjǫrþrimul*), a Valkyrie's name.

Hordaland (*Hǫrðaland*), a district in coastal western Norway.

Jotunheim (*Jǫtunheimr/Jǫtunheimar*), the "giants' home," the realm occupied by the "giants" (*jǫtnar*) and contrasted chiefly with *Ásgarð* (the realm of the gods), *Midgard* (the realm of human beings), and *Hel* (the realm of the dead).

Loddfáfnir, an unknown character addressed during the part of *Hávamál* called *Loddfáfnismál* (st. 111–37) and toward the end in stanza 162. The name occurs nowhere else in Old Norse literature, and attempts to decipher hints from the name's literal meaning ("young embracer"?) have shed no light on Loddfáfnir's identity.

Midgard (*Miðgarðr*), the "middle enclosure," the realm occupied by human beings and contrasted chiefly with *Ásgarð* (the realm of the gods), *Jotunheim* (the realm of the *jǫtnar* or "giants"), and *Hel* (the realm of the dead).

Óðin (*Óðinn*), the chief of the Norse gods, associated with wisdom, poetry, death, hanging, war, and the animals who prey on the dead (ravens, wolves, and birds of prey). Traveling under many pseudonyms in various sagas and myths, he is usually depicted as an old man with one eye, a wide-brimmed hat or concealing hood, and dressed in blue or gray garments.

Óðrerir (*Óðrerir*), a mead that makes its drinker a poet, guarded by Gunnlod and won by Óðin after he seduces her. This name is also used for its container (thus "poured from Óðrerir" in *Hávamál*, st. 140).

Rati, the name of a drill that Óðin uses to access the cave Gunnlod lives in, according to the fuller version of the Óðrerir story preserved in Snorri Sturluson's *Prose Edda*. *Hávamál*, stanza 106 seems to imply that he escapes, rather than gains entry, by this means, but disagreements of this sort between variants of one myth are exceedingly common.

Sanngríd (*Sanngríðr*), a Valkyrie's name.

Sigmund (*Sigmundr*), a prominent early hero of *The Saga of the Volsungs.*

Sinfjotli (*Sinfjǫtli*), Sigmund's son and nephew, another prominent early hero of *The Saga of the Volsungs.*

Skogul (*Skǫgul*), a Valkyrie's name.

Starkad (*Starkaðr*), a Norse hero fostered by Óðin under the name Hrosshárs-Grani and later instructed in how to sacrifice King Víkar in a scene from *The Saga of Gautrek.*

Suttung (*Suttungr*), a "giant" (*jǫtunn*), father of Gunnloð.

Svipul, a Valkyrie's name.

Thjódreyrir (*Þjóðreyrir*), a dwarf mentioned in *Hávamál* (st. 160). Nothing about him is known; there are no mentions of this name beyond this stanza.

Thór (*Þórr*), the most popular of the Norse gods during the Viking Age, the protector of Ásgarð and Miðgarð. A figure of "middle-class" interests and tastes, he contrasts starkly with the more "elite" interests of his father Óðin, as revealed in the blessings and curses, respectively, that they dispense on Starkad in a scene from *The Saga of Gautrek.* For an equally stark contrast between Thór and his father, see the poem *Hárbarðsljóð* in the *Poetic Edda.*

Urd (*Urðr*), the foremost of the Norns, three beings who determine the fate of the gods and humans. Urd's Well, located at the base of Yggdrasil's root in Ásgarð, is their home and the site where they carve fate on wooden planks, according to the poem *Voluspá* in the *Poetic Edda.*

Valhalla (*Valhǫll*), Óðin's hall, where men who die in battle are brought by the Valkyries. This spelling is the conventional anglicization of Old Norse *Valhǫll,* a compound formed from *valr* "a dead man on a battlefield" + *hǫll* "hall."

Valkyrie (*Valkyrja*), a woman employed by Óðin to retrieve dead warriors from battlefields and bring them to him in Valhalla. This spelling is the conventional anglicization of Old Norse *Valkyrja,* a compound formed from *valr* "a dead man on a battlefield" + *kyrja* "chooser."

Víkar (*Víkarr*), a king sacrificed to Óðin by Starkad (as instructed by Óðin) in a scene in *The Saga of Gautrek.*

Ynglings (*Ynglingar*), members of the medieval Norwegian royal family.

The Cowboy *Hávamál*

I first read selections from *Hávamál* in the seventh grade, in the short appendix about Norse mythology that Edith Hamilton appended to her classic book *Mythology: Timeless Tales of Gods and Heroes* (Little, Brown, 1942). I was struck right away by the tone of its down-to-earth, weather-beaten wisdom, which reminded me powerfully of the advice of my grandfather, June Crawford (1925–2009). After 2003, when I began to study Old Norse, it was only natural that *Hávamál* would continue to intrigue me, and I spent many of the subsequent years reading the entire text in the original every day in order to improve my Old Norse reading skills and, after my grandfather's death, to feel somewhat closer to a spirit so much like his own.

In January 2012, while reflecting on the connection I felt between *Hávamál*'s wisdom and his, I composed "The Cowboy *Hávamál*" as a condensation of the pragmatic wisdom of *Gestaþáttr* (the first constituent poem of *Hávamál*) into mostly five-line stanzas imitating my grandfather's dialect. It was not my intention to render this dialect phonetically in a thoroughly consistent way, but only to present an "eye dialect" of sorts, to suggest the dry tones of the accent behind the words.

While my other translation of *Hávamál* in this volume is more complete, the tone of this one seems more authentic to me. After all, the voice is that of my grandfather, sad with wisdom and wizened by experience, which I have always heard when reading this poem in the original.

1.   Use yer eyes,
       and never walk blind.
       There ain't no tellin'
       where there's someone waitin'
       to put one over on you.

2.   Don't be unkind to a wanderer.
       You know the type: Waiting,
       proud, outside your doorstep.
       Give 'im a break,
       and let 'im in.

3.   Let 'im get close to the fire,
       and have a chance
       to dry his clothes.
       He's been walkin' in the mountains,
       and that wears a man down.

4.   You know what he's lookin' for:
       Some clothes to change into,
       a few kind words, not too many,
       a chance to tell his story,
       a chance to hear what you'll say.

5.   You ought to have
       a damn sight of learnin',
       before you step outside that door.
       It's a lot easier to stay at home,
       but no one'll listen to you if you stay there.

6. Now, that ain't to say
    that you ought to be showy
    about your learnin'.
    Don't say too much
    and you'll say more o' the right things.

7. And don't ever think
    that other folks
    have nothin' to teach you, either.
    You only stand to gain
    by keeping yer ears open, too.

8. People's approval ain't nothin' you need.
    Half the time it ain't true.
    Just be sure you think you're right;
    and that you're comfortable in your own skin;
    you're all you can count on.

9. And while you should listen
    to people's advice,
    don't just do whatever they say.
    You've got a head on your own shoulders;
    use it, boy.

10. That head on your shoulders
    is the best thing you'll ever have.
    And no amount o' money
    can make up for not havin' it.
    Keep it in good shape.

11. The worst way to make yourself
    into a goddamned fool
    is to drink too much.
    Stay out o' the liquor,
    except you know yer limits.

12. Oh, folks'll say this and that,
    how much fun it is to drink and all.
    But the more you drink,
    the less you know,
    and that's a poor exchange.

13. I've been drunk, I'm not sayin' otherwise.
    Let me tell you what it's like:
    It's as if a bird hovered over your head,
    drinking more of your wits
    the more you drink.

14. Lord a'mighty, I was drunk,
    I was shamefaced drunk.
    And I didn't have myself
    near as good a time
    as if I'd gone home sober.

15. So keep quiet,
    keep your head clear,
    and don't back off from a fight.
    You'll be happier that way—
    and you'll die soon enough.

16.   You're a goddamned fool
        if you think you'll live forever
        just because you won't fight.
        Say nobody ever kills you—
        old age is no peach, either.

17.   I'll say another thing about drinkin'—
        I swear I'm nearly done:
        But just you think how much dumber
        a dumb man is after a few drinks:
        Who ever heard more awful bullshit?

18.   Travel, see the country,
        never miss a chance to get outdoors.
        You'll only get smarter
        by knowin' more people, more places,
        more ways to be a man.

19.   Accept hospitality, but don't be a jackass.
        Folk can only offer so much.
        And if you want to talk,
        just consider whether what you want to say
        matters to anybody else.

20.   A belly's a sure sign
        that a man's not in control of himself.
        Folks'll laugh if you're eatin' too much.
        Yer stomach's not yer head—
        you can put too much in it.

21.   You ever seen a fat cow?
        I mean, they're all fat, but only to a point:
        They don't eat so much they hurt themselves.
        And a cow is just about the dumbest thing
        on this damn earth.

22.   Nothin' to learn from a fella
        who won't but laugh at everybody else.
        What he ain't learned
        would do him some good:
        He's got his own faults.

23.   You should lie down to sleep
        and not think about tomorrow;
        you'll take care of it then.
        If you worry at night, you get nothing done,
        and you're in worse shape for the day.

24.   Not everybody
        who laughs with you
        is yer friend.
        Someone who won't but laugh
        hasn't thought about much.

25.   Not everybody
        who laughs with you
        is yer friend.
        It's one thing if a fella'll laugh with you,
        it's another if you can count on 'im.

26. You're a damn fool
    if you think you can just figure out
    a way out of any problem.
    It's good to think ahead,
    but sometimes things go wrong.

27. I wish more damn fools
    would just keep their mouths shut.
    If they did, we might not realize
    just how many goddamned fools
    there are in this old world.

28. Ain't ever been a single person
    who can keep his mouth shut
    when it comes to other people.
    But try not to gossip,
    even if it makes you look smarter.

29. You will talk yourself into trouble
    if you don't think before you speak:
    Hold that tongue, and think a little,
    or you'll find out that it's a long whip,
    and it's gonna hit you from behind.

30. Don't make fun of someone else,
    even if he owes you money,
    and don't pester people with questions.

31. Sarcastic people sound smart
    when they make fun of someone else.
    But making fun doesn't make you smart,
    and that's time you could be putting
    into somethin' more worthwhile.

32. A fella might be nice enough;
    there's still something
    that'll make 'im want to fight.
    Where there's more than one man,
    you'll eventually have a fight.

33. You shouldn't sit around
    and wait to eat all day.
    Go ahead and eat,
    unless you're eatin' later with a friend,
    otherwise you'll just be useless.

34. Don't concern yerself
    with anybody
    who won't repay yer friendship in kind.
    Better to walk a long way to a friend,
    than a short way to some ornery jackass.

35. Don't overstay yer welcome.
    Folks like company, but not too much,
    and start to resent a guest 'fore long.
    So git goin' after a while,
    or you'll git on people's nerves.

36. It dudn't matter where you live,
    long as you have a roof over you.
    Better to call some place home,
    even if it ain't much to look at,
    than to beg for ever'thing.

37. It dudn't matter where you live,
    long as you have a place.
    Better to call a place home,
    or you'll feel worse and worse,
    as you beg for more and more.

38. Keep yer guns close.
    I don't care what they say,
    there ain't no tellin'
    when there'll be call for 'em.
    An armed man has a shot.

39. Don't think a generous host
    wouldn't gladly take something
    in return for yer room and board.
    Never seen a man so nice
    he wouldn't like a little in return.

40. Don't save so much money
    that you don't use any of it.
    You'll die, after all,
    and it might not go to people you like.
    The world ain't aimin' to please you.

41.   Give yer friend
        a gift that'll matter to 'im:
        Weapons, clothes, you know the kind.
        This kind of giving, if he gits you back,
        will mean he'll have yer back when it counts.

42.   Be friendly
        to anybody friendly to you,
        and repay their gifts.
        Repay good with good,
        and bad with bad.

43.   Be friendly
        to anybody friendly to you;
        and to his friends, too.
        But be careful not to make friends
        with your friends' enemies.

44.   If you have a good friend,
        and really trust 'im,
        you should share yer mind with 'im,
        exchange gifts with 'im,
        visit 'im often.

45.   If you have another friend
        and don't trust him worth a spit,
        but want somethin' from 'im,
        speak kindly, but don't be surprised
        if you find yerself betrayin' that kindness.

46. Now this fella you don't trust:
    That's not to say you shouldn't talk to 'im,
    laugh with 'im, even—
    hell, who can you trust?
    But repay 'im just what he gives you.

47. I was young once, I walked alone,
    and I got lost on my way.
    It wasn't alone that I found happiness,
    but in good company, good friends;
    there's no joy in loneliness.

48. Be friendly, be brave if you're challenged,
    and don't nurture a grudge for too long.
    That's the way to spend yer life—
    not on worrying,
    not on shirking yer responsibilities.

49. Once I was walkin', I saw two scarecrows,
    and that gave me the damnedest funny thought:
    They were naked, so I'd give 'em clothes.
    They looked a damned sight better in 'em, too;
    a naked man just feels ashamed of himself.

50. Think about a pine on the edge o' town—
    once a part o' the forest, but the forest is gone,
    and now it's surrounded by pasture.
    Puts me in mind of a man no one loves—
    what's he got to live for?

51.   You might think you have a new friend,
        but just you wait five days, that'll test 'im.
        They say that a bad friendship
        burns for only five days,
        but on the sixth one it goes out.

52.   You may not have much,
        so don't give much.
        But I've won friends
        with just a bowl o' soup
        and half a loaf o' bread.

53.   A small ocean
        has small beaches,
        and small brains
        have damned little to give.
        But the world takes all types.

54.   Don't git too goddamned smart, now,
        there's a measure for ever'thing.
        And don't think it's for nothing
        that the stupid people
        tend to be the happier ones, too.

55.   Don't git too goddamned smart, now,
        there's a measure for ever'thing.
        You'll know you're gone too far
        when you can't find a thing to smile about:
        That's what wisdom's like.

56.   Don't git too goddamned smart, now,
      there's a measure for ever'thing.
      And if you think you can learn the future,
      you're a damned fool, not a wise man.
      You'll be happier not knowing anyway.

57.   You won't learn a thing
      if you never talk to folks,
      and nobody will learn anything from you.
      If you keep yer thoughts to yerself,
      you'll never turn the lead in yer head to gold.

58.   Don't sleep too late,
      that's no way to get things done.
      If you mean to do business, get goin'—
      a lazy wolf never caught a sheep,
      a sleeping man never earned a dime.

59.   Don't sleep too late,
      that's no way to get things done.
      If you're still sleepin' at sunrise,
      you're losin' the race already—
      someone's got more hours than you.

60.   You know how to measure wood
      and bark for a roof,
      and you know the way to tell the time,
      and determine the seasons.
      You know this stuff, son.

61. Don't go to see folks
    with your hair a mess and your clothes dirty.
    Put a damned shirt on, and some shoes—
    there's no shame in not having the best.
    And eat a little first, too.

62. Consider your reputation;
    if you go to town, and know nobody,
    and nobody has a whit to say about you,
    you'll be like an eagle stretching out its beak,
    but never catching a fish.

63. Now here's a fact I've learned:
    Tell a secret to one good friend,
    and that secret might stay with him;
    but tell two people your secret,
    and everybody will know pretty soon.

64. Don't think you're the goddamned smartest,
    or the toughest, or the best at anything,
    and don't let folks think you are, either.
    Otherwise you'll find out the hard way
    that someone is always better.

65. Watch what you say, son—
    what you say to other people
    is often exactly what you git from 'em.

66. There's bein' too early,
    there's bein' too late,
    and you can't always predict folks' timing.
    But try to be on time;
    that wins you more favor.

67. People ain't always sincere
    when they say they'll give you somethin';
    you don't know it for a fact
    till it's in yer hands.
    Don't take anybody at just his word.

68. A warm home is good for you,
    the sunshine is good for you,
    and your health, too, of course,
    but don't underestimate how good it is
    to live without things to say sorry for.

69. You can never lose ever'thing,
    even if yer health looks to give out any minute.
    You might still have yer kids, yer family,
    yer money, or something else—
    or better, a job well done.

70. Better to be alive, no matter what,
    than dead—
    only the living enjoy anything.
    I've seen a rich man's corpse;
    it wadn't different than a poor man's.

71. Break yer leg? You can ride a horse still.
    Lost a hand? Not yer voice, too, I reckon.
    Cain't hear? Bet you can still fight.
    There ain't a damn way any shot at life
    is worse than empty death.

72. It's good to have a son,
    or someone you can call that;
    there ain't too many men remembered
    except those as left family behind.

73. If two fight again' one, two'll probably win.
    And again, son, watch yer damn tongue.
    And never trust
    that what folks keep hidden from you
    is for yer own good.

74. The weather can change a lot in five days,
    it can change even more in a month,
    and you're a fool if you think you can predict it.
    Never trust to anything
    that's not in yer own power.

75. I've said you should listen,
    but don't listen to goddamned idiots.
    And remember: You might be poor,
    someone else might be rich,
    and neither o' you has the other to blame.

76. Cows die, friends and family die,
    you will die just the same way.
    But if you have a good reputation,
    that might survive you.

77. Cows die, friends and family die,
    you will die just the same way.
    The only thing that won't die
    is what folks say about you
    when you're dead.

78. I saw a rich man's sons,
    they had a good many head o' cattle.
    Now they're beggars in the street.
    Wealth's nothin' to count on;
    it'll leave you as soon as it finds you.

79. Now, a good thing may happen
    to a pretty stupid man,
    but that dudn't make him any better.
    He'll be just as arrogant,
    and not any smarter.

(81). Don't sing the praises
    of anything that ain't over.
    Not the day's before the night,
    not the work's before its end,
    not the man's before his death.